DEATH IN

MAGDALEN NABB

Death in Autumn

A Florentine Mystery

FONTANA/Collins

First published by William Collins Sons & Co. Ltd 1985
First issued in Fontana Paperbacks 1986

Copyright © Magdalen Nabb 1985

Made and printed in Great Britain by
William Collins Sons & Co. Ltd, Glasgow

Although this story is set very specifically in Florence
and its environs, all the characters and events in it are
entirely fictitious and no resemblance is intended to any
real person, either living or dead.

CHAPTER 1

Dawn still hadn't broken and the river water lapping the sides of the black rubber dinghy was of the same darkness as the sky except for a path of moving light coming from a lamp attached to the dinghy's side. A torch flashed a brief signal from the left and when the man in the dinghy answered it the truck parked on the bank was visible for an instant and then vanished in the blackness again. There was no point in trying to shout above the roaring of the weir below the next bridge. The man in the dinghy resumed his watch over the dark water. Things wouldn't get that much easier when dawn did come. The thick mist that hung over the river would take hours to disperse even if the mild autumn sun made an appearance, and the water level was still low so that every movement churned up mud. There were lights across the bridges and along the embankment, yellow and white points each surrounded by a little halo of mist. To the right, the centre of Florence was still shrouded in sleep and darkness. Nevertheless, there was an early morning feeling in the air, perhaps because of the few trucks that had trundled overhead towards the flower market, leaving their exhaust fumes to mingle with the muddy smells of the river.

The surface of the water broke suddenly at two points a few yards apart and two black shapes bobbed towards the path of light, where they became visible as two heads encased in black rubber. The divers had come up empty-handed for the fourth time. One of them lifted a hand to make a negative sign and then pointed down river to the next bridge. The two divers disappeared again and the man in the dinghy flashed another signal towards the bank and started up the outboard motor. It was true that they often came up there where small trees and rubbish, washed down to the city from the countryside, piled up under the arch on the left. The lights of the truck came on and began moving slowly forward, lighting up the gravelled track below the embankment wall, keeping pace with the dinghy. Even so, if the body had gone over the weir there would be nothing for it but to wait three days until it came up and was spotted by some passer-by in one of the small towns through which the Arno wound its way towards Pisa.

Unless, of course, the whole thing was a sick joke. It happened now and then. One of the divers, reluctant to go out in the dark, had said as much and suggested they wait till daylight but someone else who knew where the call had come from had soon put him right:

'I'd like to meet the person who could pull one over on Guarnaccia.'

'Never heard of him.'

'You have now. Marshal of Carabinieri over at Palazzo Pitti. Looks as dumb as an ox, southerner, but you'd have to be up early to catch him napping.'

'Well, that's just what somebody did, isn't it?'

And they had piled their equipment on to the truck in the dark, still grumbling.

In fact, it hadn't been someone up early who had claimed to have seen the body in the water but two young tourists who hadn't gone to bed, and the Marshal, his big, slightly protruding eyes red and puffy with sleep and his paunch more than usually evident beneath a half-buttoned jacket, had had a very hard time of it indeed.

In the first place they were foreigners, and after a long sweaty summer dealing with lost cameras, stolen handbags, missing children and almost-missing cars—all those narrow streets look alike but the name began with an F or maybe it was G, a street with a stone arch across and a cobbler's shop, or was that where we parked it yesterday—the Marshal and his men had had enough. Now here it was almost

October and tourists still ringing the bell at Stazione Pitti in the middle of the night. 'All right,' the Marshal had said wearily, sitting down at his desk, 'bring them in.' And he picked up the passports that the two boys on duty had brought to him. Swedish.

They were brought in. A tall bearded young man and a girl. As they came through the door the Marshal could see that their rucksacks and plastic bags almost filled the little waiting-room beyond. He motioned them to sit down and the young man said a few incomprehensible words.

'Can't you speak any Italian?'

The young man looked at his girlfriend and she took out a phrasebook.

After almost half an hour the Marshal gave up and the carabiniere who had sat down at the typewriter got up again without having written a word.

'You see how it is, Marshal,' he said. 'We kept telling them to go to Borgo Ognissanti but they kept on ringing the bell and shouting things through the speaker. They don't understand a word. I didn't want to wake you, but what could we do?'

'I'll ring Borgo Ognissanti myself.' At Headquarters there was always somebody who could cope in most languages. He would get them to tell their story over the phone and if it turned out to be anything serious the Company Captain would have to be woken.

He dialled the number, muttering to himself the way he did all through the summer, 'I don't know what they come here for, they'd do better to stay at home . . .'

It was serious. At least, it was if the story they told was true. When they had finished the Marshal got on the line again and had it repeated to him in Italian. Afterwards the Lieutenant on the other end said:

'Do you want me to call the Captain for you?'

The Marshal hesitated a moment and then said, 'Yes,' and rang off. To the two boys on duty he said, 'A body in the river. The Captain's coming over.' Then he added: 'One of you make some coffee. We're going to be all night sorting this lot out.'

It was to take longer than one night to sort out. If you counted the death of a man in New York which marked the real end of the story, it was to take almost two years.

'What time was this?'

'Between half past eleven and midnight, I think. We'd given up looking for accommodation by then. It was getting too late to be ringing doorbells and we can't really afford the sort of hotels that have night porters. We always carry sleeping-bags for emergencies so we weren't too worried.'

'You never book accommodation in advance?'

'That's not the way we travel. We'd heard of a hostel in Via Santa Monica but it turned out to be full. We tried one or two other places nearby and then started back towards the river, thinking that in the centre we'd find a bar or something that stayed open late. In fact we found one before we reached the river, just near here in Piazza Pitti. We stayed there until it closed.'

'I see. Just a moment . . .' The Captain stopped to translate so that the Marshal's boy could take down the statement. The young carabiniere typed very rapidly with two fingers. The conversation had been in English, a little stilted on both sides but adequate. Each time the typing stopped they carried on. The Captain was unshaven and not too happy at having been got out of bed at three in the morning, but although he didn't approve of foreigners rambling around the country with rucksacks and too little money, he was impressed by the seriousness and obvious intelligence of the two Swedes and more or less inclined to believe their story after some initial doubts as to whether they weren't just looking for a warm place to pass the rest of the night.

'You decided to sleep out?'

'At that point it was necessary.'

'Why the Ponte Vecchio?'

'It's a popular place to sleep for young people.'

That was true, and as a rule they slept late so that people had to pick their way through the huddled grimy sleeping-bags to get across the bridge on their way to work in the morning.

'What time did you see the body?'

'Almost directly we got there. We were leaning over the parapet, in the middle where there are no shops.'

'Why?'

'Why?'

'Why were you leaning over the parapet?'

The young man seemed surprised. 'Looking at the view, the lights on the water. It's very beautiful.'

'Was there anyone else on the bridge?'

'No, nobody.'

'You still haven't told me what time it was.'

'I didn't look at my watch, I didn't think of it, I'm sorry. But once we were sure, we came here immediately and I should think it can only be a five minute walk, so . . .'

The Captain looked beyond him at the Marshal, who was standing watching the proceedings with an expressionless face.

'Three-twenty-seven when they got here, sir.'

'Thank you. Go on, please.'

'Well, we weren't sure at first what it was. We could just make out a dark shape, under the bridge up against one of the arches There were some boulders there and it was slapping against them gently. Then it must have worked loose. Anyway it sort of rolled over and began drifting out from under the arch so that the lights from the bridge made it more visible. It was dragging along slowly as if it were scraping the river bed, so I suppose the water was low there. We saw the face and hair. Only for a few seconds because then it floated away from the light, rolled over again and sank. At least, we think it sank. We couldn't see it any more but of course it may just have been the darkness.'

Again they stopped so that the Captain could translate and the typewriter began clacking again. The Marshal's

other boy brought in more coffee. Having to go through
everything twice was making it a long business.

'What made you come here?'

'What . . . well, to report what we'd seen, I mean . . .'

'But why here, to this station? You could have phoned the
police emergency number from the nearest telephone-box.'

'I see what you mean, but no, we couldn't. We had no
telephone tokens, we only arrived here today, and you see,
we'd seen this place earlier when we were here in the Piazza.
We were having a look at the Pitti Palace and we saw your
sign and the bell, so naturally we thought of coming back.'

'I see. Can you give an account of your movements for
the whole of the day?'

'You surely don't think that we had anything to do with
this?'

'I didn't say so. Nevertheless, I need an account of your
movements. Would you mind going back into the waiting-
room for a moment? You can organize your thoughts on
that while I make a telephone call.'

When they had been taken out the Captain looked at the
Marshal and said: 'What do you think?' He had learned
over the years that it was always worth asking Guarnaccia
what he thought even if you didn't get an answer for three
days. This time he didn't have to wait so long.

'I think they're telling the truth.'

'In that case we'd better give the order for the river to be
dragged.'

'Would you like me to call, sir?'

'If you would. I'll go on dictating the statement.'

And the Marshal had telephoned.

They found the body just as dawn was breaking. There were
few people about but two or three had collected on the
bridge to watch as the divers went down with a rope and
hooks. A great swirl of mud came to the surface first, then
the two divers, then a limp and slimy form that seemed
more like a thick-pelted animal than a human being. But

when they got it to the bank and heaved it on to the gravel path it rolled sideways and a thin white limb protruded.

'Christ . . .' muttered one of the divers, ripping off his mask. 'Looks like a suicide but she must have been some sort of loony.'

The dead woman was perhaps fifty years old. She had on a lot of rings, a large bracelet and heavy pendant earrings, all thick with mud. But underneath the sopping fur coat she was quite naked.

CHAPTER 2

'Have you seen this?'

'Not in the paper but I saw the official report.'

'What a turn up, and to think it happened so long ago and it's only just come out.'

'Somebody's been clever.'

'You can say that again.'

The Marshal's boys were all agog and so was the rest of the city. Nobody had ever heard of a case quite like it. The *Nazione* gave the story almost a full page with a big photograph of the unfortunate jeweller. It seemed that a man had come into his shop and asked to see a large diamond which he intended to have set in Florence for his wife on their anniversary. He made his choice and then said he would return after a few days with his wife to decide on the setting. When he came back, accompanied by a woman, he handled the stone for a few seconds in the jeweller's presence. They made their decision and then left to go to the bank and arrange for the payment. They never came back and it was only yesterday that another customer, something of an expert, took a look at the diamond and suspected it was a fake. It was. 'All he did was look at the stone that first time,' the astonished jeweller was quoted as saying. 'And yet he had made a perfect copy and must have substituted it for the real one right under my nose. He was a cool one all right. Of course we're insured . . .'

The police had little hope of ever solving the case. The Marshal's boys, who rarely got to deal with anything more exciting than stolen handbags and smalltime drug pushers, were fascinated. None of them so much as glanced at the four lines reporting that a body had been fished out of the river, presumed to be a suicide.

The Marshal noticed it, but apart from regretting the loss of his night's sleep, he didn't give it much thought.

The Captain over at Headquarters in Borgo Ognissanti was obliged to give it a great deal of thought, though he, too, would have liked to have a go at that jewel robbery which was being dealt with by the police and Interpol. Reluctantly he put the newspaper aside and turned back to the thin file which had no name on it. They were going to have to identify the wretched woman, if only to bury her. The red tape involved in burying people was considerable and a woman had to be buried in her maiden name. He could see that body lying in its refrigerated compartment for quite some time once the post mortem was finished. After some moments' thought the Captain picked up the phone and made a call to the *Nazione*. There was a reporter with whom he was on good terms who might help him out.

'Yes?'

'Galli? Captain Maestrangelo here. I need your help.'

'What can I do for you?'

'That woman we fished out of the Arno. I need to identify her. You couldn't manage to write something a bit longer and publish a picture, could you? I'm hoping somebody might recognize her.'

'Difficult. I don't know whether the editor would wear it unless you've got something new to tell me.'

'Nothing at all, that's the trouble.'

'Then I don't see what I could write. Somebody's already reported the thing. If you get me the picture, I'll see if I can get that in, asking anybody to come forward, etcetera.'

'I need more than that. Too many people don't even buy the newspaper. I want something people will talk about, that way there's more chance that they'll pick the paper up in a bar and take a look.'

'I don't see how I can manage that if there's no story to start with. What's the problem, anyway? I thought it was just a suicide—is there some story behind it that you're not telling?'

'No. Just a red tape problem for now. The sooner we identify her, the sooner she can be buried. But as a matter of fact there's a possibility it might not be a suicide if that's any help.'

'It is. Can I say you suspect murder?'

'You can say what you like as long as you don't quote me. In any case you can surely make something of her wearing nothing but a fur coat. It's bizarre enough.'

'Not if she was just nuts, but if you suspect murder that puts it in a different light—how old was she?'

'Fiftyish.'

'Not likely to have been a tart?'

'No, though I've got a man checking that out just in case.'

'Well, I'll do my best. Makes a change you telling me to write what I want.'

'Don't you always?'

The journalist laughed and rang off.

The article came out the next day. The photographer had done his best to give some semblance of life and normality to the dead face and the journalist had made what he could of the thin story, but it was all too small.

A week passed but nobody came forward to identify the woman. The Captain's man had established that her face wasn't known among the prostitutes in the city. The fur coat she was wearing hadn't been bought in Florence, at least not from any furrier still in business, but it was rather old-fashioned anyway. The label had long since come off. The woman's matching bracelet and earrings were worthless and bore no hallmark, so were unlikely to be of any help in the identification. A house-to-house check of buildings overlooking the river upstream from the Ponte Vecchio had, as yet, produced no witness to the dumping of the body, as was only to be expected since everyone was sure to have had their shutters closed at that hour. That left the post mortem report. The Captain didn't get to read it as soon as it arrived because he was too busy. Some new faces had appeared on the drug scene and there had been two deaths, both young people, one after the other. There was little doubt that a new gang was at work, probably pushing dirty stuff. The Captain had spent all morning briefing the young plainclothes men who would mingle with the various groups of addicts until the new source was tracked down. Sooner or later an informer would talk in exchange for the price of his next fix. In the end he read the autopsy report during his lunch hour, sending down for a sandwich and a glass of wine.

He was looking for confirmation of what both he and the Substitute Prosecutor had suspected that chilly early morning on the river bank when the doctor had made his first examination. They had seen bruises on the neck and a laceration round one side.

FOR THE ATTENTION OF THE SUBSTITUTE PROSECUTOR OF THE REPUBLIC FOR FLORENCE

The undersigned Dr Maurizio Forli was, on 29th September, called by the Procura of Florence to examine the body of an unidentified corpse recovered from the river Arno. Following the external examination of the body at the point of recovery a request was made for dissection and forensic examination for the purpose of supplying information on the time and cause of death and the identification of the corpse.

In answer to specific queries received in relation to the aforementioned request:

1. Death occurred six hours before recovery of the corpse.

2. Cause of death was throttling.
3. The body is that of a female of approximately fifty years of age.

There followed an account of the external examination of the body, beginning with clothing and jewellery and noting that according to the presentation of hypostasis the victim had been naked at the time of death and had been left in a supine position for 3–4 hours after death occurred. Excoriations on the forehead and hands containing clay and grit had been caused by the rolling of the body on the river bed, the major part of the corpse being protected by the fur coat.
The signs of throttling were dealt with at greater length.

. . . pronounced cyanosis of the face . . . asymmetrical bruising accompanied by half-moon lesions, the bruising being more extensive and the lesion deeper on the left side of the neck, indicating that the aggressor was right-handed.

But it was the next paragraph which interested the Captain.

Laceration surrounded by extensive bruising on the left side of the neck suggesting the removal by violence of a heavy necklace. It should be noted:
a) The form of the laceration suggests a necklace matching the bracelet worn by the deceased.
b) The extensive bruising surrounding the laceration indicates that it occurred before death.
c) The position of the laceration indicates that it was made by a left to right movement while the victim was supine.

The Captain read the paragraph through again but still it made no sense. If the motive was robbery the attacker would have taken all the jewellery, not just one piece, and the same thing applied if robbery was a simulated motive. And if the attacker had for some reason wanted only the necklace it would have been easier to remove it after the woman's death. That only left a violent quarrel as the reason for ripping the necklace off, but it hadn't been found. The attacker had taken it with him and either kept it or thrown it in the river.

'Or maybe,' murmured the Captain to himself, 'he ripped it off because it was simply in his way.' Gradually, he was building up in his mind a picture of an exceptionally cool-headed murderer who acted quickly and calculatedly so that the victim had no warning and no chance to react, and who had calmly dressed the body in the fur coat and taken it, possibly in the passenger seat of a car, to the river.

He read through the rest of the autopsy report without much hope of finding anything helpful.

The woman had had a slightly enlarged heart, probably congenital, which would have helped her attacker in that she had probably lost consciousness very quickly after he had begun throttling her.

Stomach contained approximately 200 grammes of milk partially coagulated . . . kidneys and pancreas normal . . . reproductive organs normal . . . scar dating back fifteen to twenty years probably connected with a difficult birth . . . It should be noted:

a) that the lungs contained no water.

b) that the stomach contents carried no odour of alcohol . . .

She hadn't been too drunk to react, then. Had she been asleep? There were no marks on the body to suggest that there had been a struggle with her attacker, but if she was asleep it made no sense to rip off the necklace instead of unfastening it. The Captain sat alone, struggling to make sense of such information as he had on the unknown woman. Then he reached for the telephone.

'Get me Stazione Pitti.'

But it was Brigadier Lorenzini who answered. 'I'm sorry, sir, the Marshal's out on his hotel round.'

'Ask him to ring me when he gets in.'

'Yes, sir. He should be back any minute . . . But he was late getting off with it being Monday morning.'

'I understand.'

Monday morning was always the same. People returning late on Sunday night after a day out or a weekend away would find the house broken into or the car or the dog missing, and first thing Monday morning they would be queueing up with sheets of government-stamped paper to report the theft. It had been after eleven-thirty when the Marshal had finally managed to get away, determined to check on two boarding-houses that he kept a particular eye on. Afterwards he decided to make a brief call at a more luxurious hotel which he had to pass anyway on his way back.

The Riverside Hotel was quiet when the Marshal arrived. Lunch was being served in the main dining-room, and the blue-carpeted breakfast lounge to the right of the reception hall was empty apart from one elderly couple who were probably waiting for a taxi. Some matching luggage was stacked near the door. The receptionist, a smooth young man wearing a black silk bow tie, handed the blue register over with no other comment than a prim 'good morning'. The Marshal was on first name terms with the receptionists, proprietors and porters who received him in more modest hotels, and conducted open warfare with those of some particularly seedy ones, but here he was regarded as a necessary evil and kept at a distance. On the whole he preferred open warfare to chilly politeness. Nevertheless, the fact that he was none too welcome didn't perturb him in the least and he took his time just as he always did, reading each registration carefully with his protruding eyes that noticed everything and betrayed nothing. When he had finished he handed back the register without a word since

that was the way they did things here. A little white dog
had come out from the open door behind the desk, but the
minute the receptionist spotted it, it gave a nervous start
and disappeared again.

The Marshal made for the door where a porter in a red
and white striped jacket was loading the luggage into a taxi,
while a queue of honking cars waited impatiently behind it.
The elderly couple came out behind him.

'Just a moment!'

The Marshal went on his way assuming that someone
was calling to the departing couple, but the receptionist had
followed him out and caught up with him. He seemed
slightly embarrassed. 'Perhaps you could help with a small
problem . . .' Sooner or later people always did want help
with some problem, whether small or large, and they didn't
think twice about asking, no matter how unhelpful they had
always been themselves.

The Marshal turned and followed him back in. He gave
the man no encouragement but stood there, his face expressionless, waiting. 'It's about this dog . . .' The animal
had reappeared and was now standing with his front paws
on the lower rungs of the receptionist's stool, quivering
nervously. The Marshal looked down at it and then back at
the receptionist.

'Well?'

'Something will have to be done about it. It can't stay
here and I thought perhaps you . . . It belongs to one of our
guests—not that we normally allow animals but she's been
here years so we felt obliged to make an exception.
Nevertheless . . .'

'What do you want me to do? Arrest it?' The Marshal's
tone was dangerous. As if he had nothing else to do but
worry about a half-pint dog!

'You don't understand. Normally she takes it with her
when she goes on a trip but this time she's left it and
without so much as a by-your-leave! We really can't be
expected—'

'Have it put down or send it to the RCPCA.' The Marshal turned to leave again.

'Wait! That's what I want to know, if we have the right. If not, then when she comes back . . .'

'Leave it alone, then, it's doing you no harm.' He had reached the door but the other followed him, thoroughly agitated now.

'That's what you think! It hangs around the reception desk the whole time because the night porter's always made a pet of it. In a hotel of this class that sort of thing can't be tolerated, surely you can understand that.' He didn't add 'even though you're never likely to set foot in one as a guest' but he might as well have done. 'The manager insists I do something but I can hardly shut the animal up in her room, there's no knowing what damage . . . All I want to know is what our legal position is.'

'Ask a lawyer,' suggested the Marshal drily.

'We can't waste a lawyer's time over a thing like this; besides which, that would cost more money than getting a vet to put it down!'

'Well then, stop wasting my time and leave it be. Don't tell me in a place like this you can't afford to feed it. It's no bigger than a rabbit.'

'And if she doesn't come back?'

'Why shouldn't she come back?' The Marshal had lost hope of shaking the man off. They were on the doorstep and he kept tugging at the sleeve of the Marshal's black uniform, glancing back every few seconds to make sure he wasn't wanted inside. The taxi moved off followed by an angry chorus of hooting and the porter went inside. At this point the receptionist lowered his voice to a confidential gossipy whisper.

'Well, for one thing, I know for a fact she didn't even take a suitcase. We keep them in store in the attic for her since she's here permanently.'

'If she didn't take a suitcase,' said the Marshal, 'then she won't be gone long, will she? And now—'

'Hm. It's not my place to say . . .' He glanced over his shoulder again. 'It's not my place to say, but . . . I've never liked her . . . perfectly respectable on the surface and I've nothing against her, nothing concrete, but there's *something*. You understand what I mean? I imagine that in your job—'

'No,' said the Marshal, 'I don't understand you.' The man certainly made a better impression when he confined himself to 'thank you and good morning'.

'It's been eight days.'

'What has?'

'She's been gone eight days and a woman of that sort doesn't go away for eight days without a suitcase. Maybe she couldn't pay her bill. This month's was due. If we keep this dog and she's vanished we'll be stuck with it. Now do you understand?'

The Marshal didn't answer. He made a calculation and then walked back into the hotel with the receptionist fluttering behind him.

'Well, I'm glad to see you realize that something's got to be done. It's all very well for the manager to say—'

'Give me back the register. How old is this woman?'

'Forty-eight. Well kept, I'll admit, but—'

'Height?'

'About my height . . . What's this got to do with the dog?'

'Blonde?'

'Bleached. You know her? There, I *knew* there was something. I can always tell.'

'Where's her registration?'

'Wait, I'll find it for you . . . I just knew, it's a feeling I get . . . here.'

The Marshal looked at the information, slowly took out his notebook and copied it down carefully. He buttoned the notebook back into his pocket. 'You'll be hearing from us.'

'I do *hope* it's nothing serious,' lied the receptionist, then remembering just in time: 'What about the dog?'

'You'll probably be able to have it put down, if that's what you want.' At the doorway he couldn't resist turning to add sententiously: 'But you just might have to identify a corpse first.'

'A corpse? You mean she's . . . *Me* . . .? Oh my God!' That wiped the excited expression off his face. 'I'm afraid I'd faint . . .'

'I'm damn sure you would,' growled the Marshal to himself, going on his way.

CHAPTER 3

'I'm sorry to have kept you waiting.' Captain Maestrangelo returned to his office that afternoon to find the Marshal sitting there patiently, his big hands resting squarely on his knees. They talked for a few moments about the latest on the new drug gang. The Marshal knew the parents of one of the youngsters who had died and so had a personal as well as an official interest in the case. After a while the Captain said: 'I gather you got my message, but there was really no need to come over, I just wanted to bring you up to date on that body in the Arno affair. It's not a suicide. I spoke to the magistrate this morning . . .'

The Marshal listened carefully to a summary of the contents of the autopsy report. It wasn't until the Captain said: 'Identifying her is still going to be a real headache,' that he offered: 'There's a possibility that I've found out who she is . . .'

They didn't go immediately to the hotel since they would have to see both the day and the night staff. Maestrangelo telephoned the manager and asked for all the personnel to be present that evening at the time of the evening change-over. The response was polite but decidedly reserved.

'Am I allowed to ask why?'

'It would be better if we discussed that when I arrive.'

'He knows why,' commented the Marshal when the Cap-

tain had hung up. 'That receptionist will have told everybody in the place.'

It was already dark by the time their car crossed the
bridge under which the body had been recovered, and a
drizzly rain was falling into the river. There was so much
traffic clogging the narrow streets at that hour that it was
fortunate the hotel had an underground garage beside the
entrance.

As it turned out, the Marshal had been right. The receptionist had told everyone in the place. There was an atmosphere of mild excitement when the carabinieri were shown
into the manager's crowded office, but nobody seemed un-
duly worried or tense apart from the receptionist himself,
whose name was Guido Monteverdi and who kept edging
up to the Marshal at every opportunity to give some new
reason why he was the least appropriate person to identify
the body. The Marshal was relieved that it was the Captain
who took his statement while he himself took that of the
night porter, a quietly spoken, pleasant man in his late
thirties who did his best to be helpful without resorting to
gossip. He and the Marshal sat facing each other across a
cluttered desk in the small office where the hotel's accounts
were kept, and from where the usual noises of the hotel were
only just audible. The porter gave his name as Mario Querci
and answered the routine questions about his birth and place
of residence. Then he began to speak of the missing guest.

'No, I wouldn't say she was a happy woman. She often
seemed to me disappointed with life, a little bitter, but she
never seemed moved to do anything about it. I suppose a
lot of people are like that.'

The Marshal, watching him as he spoke, wondered if the
night porter himself wasn't like that, too. You didn't often
find a fairly presentable, youngish man in a job of that sort.
More often than not they were retired men, or none too
healthy ones who found the work easy to cope with. Perhaps
in this class of hotel such people weren't acceptable. He
made no comment but let the other go on talking.

'I always felt that she'd had some real disappointment at one time and that it had embittered her.'

'Did she say so?'

'No . . . nothing specific. But it might be the case, even so. There could have been something that happened a long time ago in her own country. She'd been living here about fifteen years and I've only been here for eight, so . . .'

'Where were you before?'

'In a hotel further north. I suppose, more than anything, it was the fact that she had trouble sleeping that gave the impression that she was unhappy.'

'She had trouble sleeping so she came down here and passed the time away chatting to you, is that it?'

'Yes . . .' He seemed embarrassed.

'Well, I suppose in your job you're bound to listen a good deal to people's problems whether you want to or not.' He was typical, the Marshal thought, of the sort of porters, waiters and barmen whom everyone calls by their first names and who are always willing to do small favours in an unaffected way, always with a friendly, conspiratorial smile. 'What about visitors?'

'She never had visitors, though she wasn't alone in the world, I know that.'

'How?'

'There were letters, not often but fairly regularly. I take the post in before I leave in the morning.'

'Letters from her own country?'

'No, I can't think there was ever one from Germany, at least, not that I remember, though there could have been, I suppose, without my noticing or on my night off. They came from all over the world. She wrote letters, too.'

'In answer to the ones she received?'

'I don't know . . . No, I think they always went to Germany. You'd have to ask the receptionist; she'd leave them with him during the day if she didn't go out and post them herself.'

'Did she go out much?'

'I don't think so. Again, you should check with the day staff. She did go away occasionally for a few days.'

'Had she been away recently?'

'No, not for over a year, if I remember rightly.' He hesitated a moment and then said: 'I told you she never had visitors and she didn't as a rule, but . . .'

'Well?'

'Well, you could hardly call him a visitor—I mean, he didn't go up to her room as you might be thinking—but there was a man who came in and asked for her, a very respectable-looking man, tallish, well-dressed. She came down and met him here and they went out together.'

'At night, presumably, if you saw him?'

'Yes. I suppose about elevenish.'

'When was this?'

'It must be nearly a month ago.'

'You're sure?'

'I can't be sure to the day. He didn't come back with her and since he wasn't registered here I've no way of checking.'

'You're sure it wasn't the night she disappeared?'

'Oh, quite sure. It was well before that . . . Would you mind if I asked you something?'

When the Marshal nodded his consent the porter went on: 'I just wanted to . . . well, to know what happened. You said she was found in the river but you didn't say—was it suicide?'

'No.'

'I see.' He seemed almost relieved.

The Marshal waited but the porter asked nothing further so he went on: 'Did she confide in you, things of a personal nature?'

'She talked a lot about her health. Despite her insomnia she hardly ever took anything, sleeping pills, that sort of thing. She was very concerned about her diet, too. I don't mean the way women usually are, worrying about keeping slim. She was very slim anyway.'

'Yes,' murmured the Marshal. When he had arrived on the river bank that morning with the Captain the first thing he had noticed had been one thin bluish leg issuing from the sodden fur.

'She went in for those health food things. She talked a lot about wheat germ and vitamin C. She even gave me some vitamin C tablets once, saying that if you spend a lot of time in a confined space and don't get enough fresh air—I'm sorry, that's of no interest to you, I suppose, but she talked that way a lot.'

'To be honest,' the Marshal said, 'I was thinking of things of a more personal nature than that. This man who came, for instance, she didn't tell you anything about him or about any other men?'

'No . . . She never talked about men except in general terms. But . . .'

'But what?'

'Well, there must have been a man in her life but I was never clear about whether he was in the past or the present.'

'It doesn't sound as if he was still around if she never received him here.'

'Well, there were the trips she took, of course, but she always talked about it in the past tense in a way that's difficult to explain. She didn't talk about *him*, as I said, but about another woman.'

'Someone she was jealous of?'

'That's putting it mildly. You'd have to have known her to understand. She always had this calm, ironic sort of attitude, about herself, about everything. She could be very scathing, hard in a way, but in an amusing way. I'm not very good at expressing things but if I say that her main concern seemed to be her health—well, obviously, she took it seriously because she was very rigid about her diet and these health pills—but when she talked about it, it didn't come out as serious. She always talked about herself and about everything else in a sort of detached, ironic way. I'm making her sound a bit unpleasant but she wasn't really, though people who didn't know her so well might have thought so.'

The Marshal had already talked to a chambermaid and a waiter who both thought so, but he only said: 'You were telling me about her being jealous.'

'That's just it. When she talked about this other woman, that was the only time she showed any real emotion. She still tried to keep the same ironic tone but even so it was obvious that underneath there was real fury. There were times when she said some really bitchy things. She would almost let herself go completely, though never for long.'

'What sort of things did she say?'

'It was always more or less the same story. It seems the other woman was older and she harped on that. She'd say something like: "That witch is eight years older than me and she drinks like a fish. The one thing I'm sure of is that she'll die before I do. And I know for a fact that if it hadn't been for her so-called perfect English he wouldn't have given her a second glance . . ." Then she would get control of herself and change the subject.'

'What did she mean by "she'll die before I do"? Did it sound like some sort of threat?'

'No, not at all. She seemed certain of it, that's all. I always got the impression that she kept herself healthy because of this other woman.'

'You mean that's how she intended to outlive her?' The Marshal's big, slightly bulging eyes bulged even more.

'You'd have to have known her to understand,' repeated the porter quietly. 'She was a very determined woman in her own way.'

'Hmph.' The Marshal pondered on this for a moment and then added, 'But she didn't succeed, by the look of it.'

Over an hour later, back in the manager's more spacious office, he and the Captain sat alone comparing notes. With the exception of the night porter, Mario Querci, the dead woman had been little known and even less liked by the hotel staff.

There was no doubt that the missing guest was the woman they had fished out of the river; all of them had recognized the photograph of the dead woman. If nobody had come forward to identify her it was because the hotel manager took the *Corriere della Sera* more often than the *Nazione* and the rest of the staff, if they bothered to read the newspaper at all, read his. None of them had seen the article, so Galli's efforts had been in vain. Two and a half hours of questioning had produced little enough useful evidence, but at least the woman now had an identity.

Hilde Vogel had been born in Germany and was forty-eight years old, slim, artificially blonde, unostentatiously well-dressed. She sent a registered letter to Germany once a month and took a trip abroad approximately once every two years, booking her flight through the receptionist who had repeated to the Captain that he knew there was something, he could always tell, but that it was really the manager's place to identify the body. She had last been seen at dinner eight days ago. Nobody had seen her leave the hotel, not even Querci, the night porter, despite his position in the entrance hall, and there was no other exit. The back of the hotel overhung the river.

Both the Captain and the Marshal were tired and hungry. When they emerged from the office into the reception area they were reminded of their hunger by a faint but delicious smell coming from the main dining-room where some guests were still eating, judging by discreet noises of cutlery.

Mario Querci was at his post, advising a middle-aged couple about a day trip to San Gimignano and Siena. 'If you like I'll telephone the bus station for you . . .'

He looked up and smiled as the two carabinieri appeared. 'All finished?'

'I'm afraid not,' the Captain said. He didn't like to add that they were about to join the men who were examining the dead woman's room, because of the presence of the guests who, anyway, were too busy trying to translate the price of the coach tickets into dollars to take any notice of the uniformed men.

'That receptionist, Monteverdi . . .' said the Captain as they went up the blue-carpeted stairs because the lift had just started up.

'Hmph.' The Marshal refrained from further comment.

They trod silently along more blue carpet looking for Room 209. Silk-shaded lamps were lit on low, half-moon tables all along the corridor. 209 was halfway along facing the lift doors.

'It's going to cost us a lot of time and manpower to check the backgrounds of all the staff, but I suppose we can be thankful that she had no contact with any of the other guests.'

'So they say—' the Marshal sounded unconvinced—'and I suppose it's true since they were all agreed about it. But as for the rest . . . It won't do. It won't do at all.'

'I must say I had the feeling that the manager had something to hide.'

'And he wasn't the only one.'

CHAPTER 4

209 was a small suite with sitting-room, bedroom and bathroom. In the sitting-room, which was furnished in yellow and white, the fingerprint technician was already packing his things to leave.

'Pretty much a waste of time,' he remarked, looking up as the Captain entered with the Marshal following behind. 'The room's been cleaned and there's hardly a clear print in the place. The manager had said, "Of course the room was cleaned, there was no reason to think anything was wrong." '

Well, nothing could be done about it now.

Two of the Captain's men were at work in the bedroom,

one of them going through the pockets of the clothes in the wardrobe, the other sorting and packing the documents he had found in the smaller drawers of the dressing-table.

'I'll take the documents. Put them in an envelope.' The Captain was looking about him. After a while he muttered a curse under his breath. Not only had this room, too, been cleaned, but anything that had been out of place had been put away. They had nothing but the chambermaid's vague description to help them reconstruct what might have happened there, and she had little to say other than that the bed had been unmade and a few clothes strewn about, a normal enough state to find a bedroom in at that hour of the morning.

'What time was it exactly?' the Marshal had asked her.

'Nine o'clock. I always took her breakfast up at that time.'

'And you didn't think of telling anyone that she wasn't there?'

'Who should I have told? There was nothing to stop her going out early if she felt like it. I get paid just the same whether she eats the stuff or not—and don't imagine she ever gave me a tip because she didn't.'

'So then you tidied the room?'

'A bit.'

'What do you mean a bit?''

'A bit. Enough so's the cleaner could come in.'

'And when did you finally think of telling somebody she was missing?'

'Next morning, I think. Or it might have been the morning after.'

'You told the manager?'

'No.'

'Who did you tell, then?'

'Gino.'

'Who's Gino?' The Marshal felt like giving her a good shaking.

'He waits on her table. He must have said something about her not turning up to meals.'

'Why should you tell this Gino and not the manager? Is he your boyfriend?'

'What's it got to do with you?'

And to cap it all, when the Marshal had asked her if she hadn't seen Hilde Vogel's picture in the paper she had simpered and said: 'I only read the horoscopes.'

'We're ready to go,' said one of the Captain's men. 'We'll seal the place up unless there's anything further you need to do here.'

'No . . . no, carry on.' The Captain picked up a crystal perfume spray from the dressing-table and put it down again next to a hairbrush from which the technician had already removed a few blonde hairs. There was little point in hanging on there. The magistrate had given orders for seals to be put on the door and windows. He could always come back and search the room again when he had more idea of what to look for. Perhaps the documents they were taking away would tell him something.

'Do you need me any more?' the Marshal asked as they went down in the lift.

'No. I'll drop you off at Pitti, you should get something to eat. But I may need you or even a couple of your boys from tomorrow. With so many of my men occupied on this drug case, all the checking up that's going to be necessary on this job will be a problem.'

When they stepped out of the lift in front of the reception desk, Mario Querci looked up from a stack of breakfast orders and said: 'If your car's in the garage you'd better carry on down in the lift. It's raining hard.'

'We don't need a key? We tried to come up that way but we couldn't open the lift doors.'

'Only residents have the key for coming up that way but you can open the doors from the inside.'

'Thank you. Good night.'

'Good night.'

It was raining so hard that it was difficult to distinguish

more than a misty blur of yellow and white lights, even with the windscreen-wipers going their fastest.

'The river will soon fill up if this keeps on for a few days,' observed the Marshal as they drove along the embankment as far as the Ponte Vecchio and turned left towards the Palazzo Pitti where he got out.

When the car reached Borgo Ognissanti the carabiniere on duty in the guards' room pushed the button to start the inner gate sliding back and indicated to the Captain that the heavy young man with his hands deep in his raincoat pockets and a cigarette in his mouth was waiting for him. The Captain wound down his window and recognized Galli, from the *Nazione*.

'I'll be calling a press conference tomorrow.'

'That's what I thought,' said Galli, grinning.

'All right, you can come up.' One good turn deserved another.

Only the main corridors were lit in that part of the building but in the opposite wing, beyond the lawns and the colonnade of the old cloister, there were lights burning in a ground floor room where the younger men who were off duty were playing pingpong before going up to their dormitories.

The Captain unlocked his office door, switched his desk lamp on and slid the large envelope he was carrying into a drawer.

'So you were right,' Galli began, dropping into a big leather chair. 'It wasn't a suicide.' He had evidently eaten and drunk fairly heavily and his face was pink and cheerful. He stubbed out his cigarette in the clean ashtray on the desk and fished in his mackintosh pocket for a fresh packet. 'I'm soaked through. I hope I'm not ruining your chair. What can you tell me?' Galli had never been known to produce notebook and pencil during an interview, but although he always appeared to be mildly drunk he made fewer mistakes than any of his colleagues.

'How much do you know already?'

'Plenty. I've had a chat to a friend of mine who works at the Medico-Legal Institute and I've been to the Riverside Hotel.'

'Sometimes I think you must follow me round all day.'

'Sometimes I do.'

'And when do you find time to write?'

'When you've gone to bed.' Galli grinned happily. 'I should be able to get this article into tomorrow's late edition.'

The Captain gave him the relevant points from the autopsy and details of the dead woman's identity.

'Suspicions?'

'I can't give you anything on that yet. It's too soon.'

'Well, this will be enough. The main thing is that we'll publish first, pull one over on the lot of them. Thanks a lot, Captain.' And, sticking another cigarette into his mouth, he went off cheerfully into the rainy night.

The Captain took the envelope full of personal documents from the drawer and tipped its contents on to the desk. Then, remembering his hunger and that he might well have to work far into the night, he got up and went to get himself a sandwich and a glass of wine from his quarters.

The lights had gone out down in the recreation hall. On his way back to his office he paused to look in on the men in the radio room since theirs was the only light burning on that floor.

'Everything all right?'

'All quiet, sir. There's nobody out on a Monday night in this weather—except us.'

Back in his office the Captain began to sort through the documents, picking up the grey passport first as he was curious to see a photograph of Hilde Vogel when she was alive. Probably it wasn't a good likeness, passport photographs rarely are, but it was evident from the fineness of the features that she had been very good-looking when young. Not pretty, the face was too severe for that, but certainly elegant and attractive. There was a hint, too, of the ironic smile mentioned by some of the hotel staff.

'So what were you up to,' murmured the Captain to himself, looking back into the cold bright eyes, 'to come to such a sticky end . . .?' But the face was secretive and told him nothing. He put the passport aside.

There were some share certificates which he was unable to read but which he could guess were in a German steel company. These he placed in a separate folder to be translated and checked as to their value.

A diary, leather bound and bearing the label of a well-known Florentine papermaker, told him little of interest. Hilde Vogel visited a hairdresser in the city centre once a week. She occasionally wrote herself a reminder to buy tights and other small items. The hairdresser's number was in the alphabetical list along with that of a doctor whose surgery was in Via Cavour and a lawyer whose offices were in Piazza della Repubblica. There was no German address to which she might have written those letters once a month. But the letters had been registered. The Captain searched through the pile of papers until he found what he was looking for: an envelope containing the brown printed carbon copies, receipts for the monthly letters. They were divided into years and the twelve receipts for each year paperclipped together. But the ones for the current year only went up to July, a date which did not coincide with one of her trips or with the brief visit of the man described by Querci, the night porter. The recipient's name was H. Vogel and the address was a bank in Mainz, West Germany. The sender was H. Vogel, Villa Le Roveri, Greve in Chianti. Whose address was that? Could she have been sending herself money to be deposited in a German account? There was no cheque-book among the papers, but then, the Captain realized, they hadn't found a handbag in the room, apart from those wrapped in polythene in the wardrobe. Probably the attacker had thrown that into the river, too, and it would be pretty well impossible to find it. The cheque-book was no doubt inside it along with her keys which had not been found either. He made a note to check all the banks in the city where she might have had an account and then replaced the letter receipts in their envelopes.

Next he examined a police permit which was up to date and which gave Hilde Vogel's place of residence as Greve in Chianti, not the Riverside Hotel in Florence. The next thing he picked up offered an explanation. It was a plastic folder containing a thick stack of contracts for the rent of a country villa near Greve in Chianti. Hilde Vogel was the owner and the villa was, as all the identical contracts stated, her only property and place of residence in Italy. The place had been rented over the past ten years to dozens of tenants for periods of one month to two years for tourist purposes only. The conveyance documents contained in the same folder showed that Hilde Vogel had inherited the property from her father twelve years previously. But if she had been staying at the Riverside Hotel for fifteen years then she had never lived in it.

The Captain selected those contracts still current and then locked all the rest of the documents back in his drawer. Someone would have to go out and take a look at that villa tomorrow. Hilde Vogel might never have lived there but it would be worth taking a look at whoever was there now. The only trouble was that he had no idea how he could spare anyone to do the job.

'Well, at least it's stopped raining,' muttered the Marshal to himself as he took the left fork towards Greve in Chianti, under a soft blue autumn sky. It was all very well, but by the time the Captain had called him that morning he was already breaking his head over the daily orders because two of his men were on duty over at the assize courts. But all he had said on the telephone was: 'I'd better go myself, sir. The only two lads I could spare are too young and inexperienced.'

'I hope I'm not causing you difficulties?'

'No, no . . .' And he had buckled on his holster and fished out the sunglasses he was forced to wear because his eyes were allergic to sunshine.

He stopped at the Carabiniere Station at the bottom of the sloping piazza in the village of Greve to get exact directions for finding the villa, and perhaps some information about the tenants.

'A right funny bunch,' the Marshal of Greve told Guarnaccia over a quick coffee at the bar nearby. The shoppers passing in front of the open door looked busy and cheerful, perhaps because of the sunshine. There was a smell of fresh bread and wood smoke mingling with the aroma of the coffee. 'But we've never had any trouble with them. Do you want me to come with you?'

'No, no. I shan't do more than take a look at the place and find out if any of the tenants know the owner. You don't know her? A Signora Vogel, German.'

'I knew the previous owner, he was German, but he died long since. The villa's let through an agency—you can see their offices across there under the colonnade between the baker's and the newsagent's. Do you want me to have a talk to them?'

'If you're not too busy?'

'We don't get many crime waves in Greve. I've got to visit an old dear who reports her next-door neighbours for one reason or another every day, but I can call at the agency after that. Come and see me on your way back. It's a beautiful place, that villa, but you'll see it's been neglected.'

It was a beautiful place. The Marshal got out of his car, took a deep breath of warm air and looked about him. The villa had large gardens around it, and beyond that it was surrounded by a mature oak wood where brilliant autumn colours contrasted strongly with the misty hills that stretched to the horizon, but a lot of the ochre-washed stucco had crumbled from the villa's façade and one of the peeling shutters on the first floor was hanging askew. Although it wasn't more than five or six minutes' drive from the village there was an almost unnatural silence. So much so that the Marshal was startled by a large wet leaf that brushed his shoulder and fell to the ground with a soft pat. The damp earth was deep in rotting yellow, red and brown leaves which nobody must ever have tried to clear away. The Marshal trod through them round to the back of the building. There was a swimming pool there but it had no water in it. A lot of the tiles were missing and it, too, was strewn with fallen leaves.

The silence was suddenly broken by a trill of music, followed by a pause and then a tune played very softly. The music came from a ground-floor room where the shutters and the window were open. The Marshal walked towards it and stood looking in. It was the kitchen. It was large and had a wooden table in the middle surrounded by straw-bottomed chairs. On one of these a fair-haired young man sat playing the flute. When he saw the big, uniformed man in dark glasses he continued playing, staring at him all the while. The Marshal stood there staring back, his huge eyes taking in everything, from the young man's expensive-looking skiing sweater to the water coming to the boil on the cooker.

'Can I help you?'

The young man was still playing. It was someone else who had spoken, someone who had come round the side of the building and joined the Marshal outside the window. A second young man, little more than a boy, thin and brown-haired, dressed in jeans and an old tweed jacket.

'I saw your car,' he stated when the Marshal turned to look at him, but the statement had the tone of a question.

'I'm making routine enquiries,' the Marshal said, 'regarding the owner of this villa, Signora Hilde Vogel. Do you know her?'

'No. I rented through an agency. They put an advert in *The Times*.'

'In the . . .?'

'*The Times*. The London newspaper.'

'I see. You're English. How long have you been here?'

'Almost a year. I paint.' He seemed to consider this an ample explanation since he added nothing further. The young man in the kitchen was still playing, watching them quizzically over his flute.

'A friend of yours?' the Marshal asked, indicating the musician.

'No. He's just arrived here. His name's Knut. He's from Norway. I don't know anything about him except that his English isn't up to much.'

'Does he speak Italian?'

'I've no idea. Would you like me to ask him?'

'Yes.'

The English boy had a certain diffidence which might be taken for politeness, but despite a strong accent and imperfect grammar he spoke Italian with a languid assurance that the Marshal found almost insolent though he couldn't have explained exactly why. He was talking to the flautist now, but the latter only shook his head very slightly and went on playing.

'Ask him if he knows the owner of this villa,' persisted the Marshal.

This time the music stopped and the young man said something and shrugged his shoulders before resuming his playing.

'No, he rented through the agent, as I did.'

'Which of you is John Sweeton?'

'I'm John Sweeton,' replied the English boy, correcting the Marshal's pronunciation.

The Marshal took out his notebook.

'And Graham . . .' He couldn't get his tongue round the surname but John Sweeton put in immediately:

'Graham didn't stay much more than a couple of weeks, though he arrived in July about the same time as Christian. He paid up the rest of the rent on his room according to the contract and then went off to Greece.'

'Who's Christian?' The name wasn't on the Captain's list of tenants.

'I don't know his surname. He's staying here on and off.'

'Is he here now?'

'No, he isn't.'

'When do you expect him back?'

'I've no idea. He comes and goes as he pleases like the rest of us.'

The Marshal was beginning to feel out of his depth and was inclined to agree with his colleague. A right funny bunch.

'He did say he was coming back?'

'Why should he say anything? His things are still here so I presume he'll be back, that's all.'

'Why doesn't he have a contract like the rest of you?'

'You'd have to ask him. Maybe he does know the owner.'

The Marshal said nothing. His big eyes were again roving over the kitchen and its contents.

'If you want to come in and look around,' said Sweeton, following his glance, 'feel free.'

'I don't have a warrant.'

Sweeton shrugged. Despite this remark of the Marshal's, he showed no curiosity as to why inquiries were being made about the owner. After a moment's hesitation the Marshal decided to go in. Sweeton took him round the place in a disinterested way.

'Nobody ever uses these ground-floor rooms much. Most of us keep to our own rooms.'

Most of the shutters were closed and the Marshal took off his sunglasses to see better in the gloom. The reception rooms were well, if sparsely, furnished with heavy antiques. The red-tiled floors were dusty and there were tiny mounds of sawdust under the furniture, showing that woodworm had been at work. Everything smelled musty. The stairs and banisters were in smooth grey stone.

'My room.' The bed was unmade and there were paintings

stacked against the walls. A badly painted modernistic landscape was propped on an easel. On the floor beside it stood a flask of wine and a glass. 'I was working when you arrived. The room next to mine was Graham's. It's empty now. I suppose Knut will take it. Do you want to look?'

'No.'

'The bathroom's up those two stairs.'

Some modernization work had been started in the bathroom and left unfinished. Tiles had been removed from the walls, leaving the cement bare. The fitments were green except for a very old-fashioned white bath with rust marks where the tap had dripped for years.

'Christian's room is on the other side of this landing. None of the others rooms are in use.' The Marshal only glanced in at the door which had been left slightly ajar. Christian's bed was made and the room was fairly orderly. There were a lot of paperback books. In the few seconds that he stood there looking in, the Marshal managed to take in everything. What he couldn't be sure of was whether John Sweeton had noticed what he had noticed. There was no way of telling from his attitude. Nevertheless, the Marshal saw what he saw. A leather belt dangling from the bedside cabinet, and beside it the two shrivelled halves of a lemon. The other things were probably hidden behind a stack of paperbacks, but even without seeing them the Marshal knew they were there.

CHAPTER 5

'So I called on the Marshal at Greve on my way back.'

'Could he tell you anything?' The Captain's voice on the other end of the telephone sounded tired. In fact, he had stayed up practically the whole night waiting for his young plainclothes men to come in from their round of the piazzas and bars where they mingled with drug addicts in the hope of finding the new supplier.

'Well, he'd had a talk to the agent who said he'd been instructed not to let again once the present contracts ran out. It seems the place was to be restored. Apart from that, he could only repeat that they had never had any trouble with these youngsters. It seems they keep themselves to themselves and there have never been complaints from anyone about them. Of course, they're in a very isolated spot so they could get up to anything without anybody knowing.'

'And you think they're up to something?'

'I'm sure that one of the ones who's staying there now is on heroin. I had a quick look at his room and got a glimpse of the usual stuff lying about.'

'Did you talk to him?'

'He wasn't there. He comes and goes and nobody knows exactly where he is. We could have a talk to him when he gets back—incidentally, he wasn't on your list of tenants whose contracts you found, so it would be worth having a word with him in case he knew the owner and is staying there under some friendly arrangement, though of course he could just be a squatter. I've asked the Marshal out there to keep an eye on the villa and let me know when the boy turns up.'

'Good. If there's nothing else . . .'

'Just one thing, sir,' persisted the Marshal slowly, pausing to get the images and words in order. He didn't like the goings-on in that villa one bit but he was having difficulty explaining his disquiet.

'Well?'

'There was another boy . . . Graham something, you gave me his name . . .'

'Allenborough. You think he may be an addict, too?'

'He wasn't there. He's left . . .'

'I see. So only one of them was there?'

'No . . . there was another, a Norwegian who's just arrived . . .' Again the Marshal felt out of his depth. 'What I'm trying to say is that this Graham who left . . . the English boy said he'd paid up the rent due according to the contract and gone off to Greece, just like that. You told me how high the rent was so I thought it was a bit funny, going off like that . . .' He wasn't explaining himself at all.

'No doubt,' the Captain said patiently, 'they're young people from wealthy families who can afford to do as they please.'

The Marshal gave it up, adding only: 'I'll send you my written report. Nothing new on the hotel staff?'

'We're still checking up on them but it's a long business and I can't spare more than one man to work on it. He hasn't come up with anything of interest yet. In the meantime, I've been in touch with Signora Vogel's lawyer, who's Swiss He's going to call me back after getting in touch with the bank in Mainz tomorrow morning. It would be a help if you could visit her hairdresser—it's on your hotel route, in Via Guicciardini. His name's Antonio.'

It would be, thought the Marshal glumly, another one like that receptionist.

'I'll try and get there before they close this evening.'

But when he rang off his thoughts returned to the villa with its smell of rotting leaves outside and mustiness inside. The sound of the flute in all that silence, and the self-assurance of the English boy who couldn't have been more than nineteen or twenty. And those telltale signs by the other boy's bedside, the dangling belt and the shrivelled lemon.

He got up slowly from his desk, buttoned up his jacket and took his holster from the hook behind the door. He didn't like it one bit and he was gradually beginning to decide why. Because if they were all from such well-to-do families they should surely be at home, studying or working, making a career for themselves with all the advantages they had. Instead of which they were drifting about wasting their time and drugging themselves like the poor unemployed wretches who hung about the city centre. Like the lad who

had died from a bad dose two weeks ago and whose parents
he knew. He decided, as he called to Brigadier Lorenzini
that he was going out again, that he would call on the
parents on his way to see the hairdresser.

'Antonio!'

'What is it?'

'Somebody to see you!'

The stifling atmosphere laden with the smells of wet hair
and hot shampoo started the Marshal sweating before he
had been in the place two minutes. And the reflections of a
dozen pairs of eyes staring at him from mirrors all over the
room didn't help. Among all that flimsy pink and blue nylon
he felt more than usually conscious of his own bulk and that
of his heavy black uniform, and he didn't know where to
put himself so as not to be in the way of all the bustling
assistants with their trays and towels.

Antonio finally appeared. He wasn't wearing an overall
like the girls but a navy polka dot shirt and a pale blue silk
scarf knotted round his neck.

'Can I help you?'

'Is there somewhere we could talk?' the Marshal asked,
shifting himself as a woman was led past him, her head
wrapped in pink towels.

'There's nothing wrong? If it's the woman in the flat
upstairs again complaining about my using all the water—'

'No, no . . . it's about one of your clients, but I'd rather
we—'

'Of course! The Vogel woman!'

'You know all about it?'

'The wife of the manager at the Riverside has her hair
done here. She came yesterday. In fact, it was she who first
recommended Signora Vogel to come to me—just a minute
. . . Caterina! Is Signora Fantozzi dry?'

'Another five minutes.'

'I'll be in the back for a moment—No, don't rinse yet, that
colour needs another two minutes. Go and comb out the

little girl. This way . . . Marshal, is it? I don't have an office but perhaps Mariannina has a cubicle free . . .'

A manicurist looked up from soaking an elderly lady's hand in a small bowl. 'Number two's free. I've just switched the wax off.'

'That's fine. This way, Marshal.'

The cubicle was so tiny there was barely room for the two of them to stand beside the narrow bed with a paper sheet on it. There was a strong smell of hot beeswax coming from an odd-looking contraption in the corner. Fortunately, Antonio turned out to be much more sensible than he looked, quite the opposite of the receptionist at the Riverside.

'I don't know how I can help,' he began.

'By telling me anything you know about her. We're trying to establish what sort of life she lived, who she mixed with.'

'Hm. Difficult. She always struck me as a loner.'

'No men?'

'Well, not from the way she talked . . .'

'What way?'

'Ironic. I don't know . . . a little bitter. She took good care of herself. She came here every week, for example, as I suppose you must already know, but I remember once she said she wondered why she bothered at times— joking, you understand—and that she was thinking of going into a convent if things didn't improve. She often talked that way.'

'But without explaining why?'

'Exactly. You wouldn't believe the way some women talk, they tell me everything, but she was rather secretive, just came out with odd remarks like that one.'

'Did you know she owned a villa out near Greve?'

'Now that she did tell me. A long time ago, I'd almost forgotten. It occurred to me at the time to wonder why she didn't live there; in fact, I asked her but she didn't seem keen on being out in the country on her own, which is understandable.'

'Did she say who did live there?'

'I think she said it was rented but I've no idea to whom. It really was a long time ago.'

'You can't think of anything else, anything at all?'

Antonio hesitated.

'Even if it seems of no importance to you, it could be useful to us,' the Marshal encouraged him.

'It isn't that . . . it's just that it's gossip, really. In my job I listen to everybody but I don't repeat. I dislike gossip.'

'In this case gossip might help us to find out who killed her and why.'

'You mean it's really true what the manager's wife told me? That you think she was murdered?'

'Yes.'

'I see. In that case . . . It was a woman who has a regular appointment at about the same time as Signora Vogel. She told me she'd seen her in a restaurant with a young man. A very young man, practically a boy. They gave the impression of being fairly intimate. They were whispering, she said. I'd rather you didn't quote me as telling you that—I mean to the newspapers and so on. I can give you the woman's name and you can talk to her yourself if you think it's important.'

'Thank you.'

A young man, practically a boy. The Marshal was thinking again of the villa, and he was liking it even less.

'How long ago was this?'

'I can tell you exactly, it was August 27th. I rarely go to restaurants since my husband died but my son insisted on taking me that day because it was my birthday—that's why I'm sure of the date.'

'A month before she died.'

'That's right. I apologize for keeping you in the kitchen but I have to see to the supper.'

The eight o'clock television news was on in the adjoining dining-room where a table was set for two. Everything in the apartment seemed as orderly and calm as the woman who was now putting a clear soup to heat. She didn't strike the Marshal as a gossip.

'Did you get a good look at the young man?'

'Not really. Signora Vogel hadn't seen me and I didn't want to stare and draw attention. She might have been embarrassed.'

'Nevertheless, you told Antonio about it.'

'You're right. I suppose I oughtn't to have mentioned it. It was only because she was late for her appointment and he was saying that perhaps she'd taken her own advice and gone into a convent—it was a joke she'd made to us the week before. I didn't see any harm in telling him; after all, she had a right to do as she pleased. But the young man seemed hardly more than a boy, which I admit I found a bit shocking. You understand?'

'Yes.'

'I suppose it's having a son about that age which made me find it distasteful. She was a little younger than I am, I imagine, but even so . . . Do you think all this has something to do with what happened to her?'

'I don't know.'

'I wish you'd sit down.'

'Don't worry. I don't want to disturb you any longer than I have to.'

'You must think me very rude but we eat at very regular hours because of my son. He's in his second year at university studying architecture but since my husband died he's had the business to look after as well. It's only a small firm of heating engineers but he has to be there practically all day, which means he studies late into the night. That's why I like to have supper ready as soon as he gets in. I do apologize. I just have a salad to prepare. I don't know what else I can tell you . . .'

'Anything you remember about what the young man looked like. You must have noticed something about him even without staring.'

'Ah yes . . . Well, I do remember he was tall and slim—at

least, since he was sitting down it was probably his slimness that gave the impression he was tall.'

She turned down the light under the soup which had begun to boil and added a pinch of salt to it.

'What about the colour of his hair?'

'Fairish, I think . . . maybe light brown, but I can't say for sure.'

'You didn't catch anything they were saying?'

'No, but . . . well, I got the impression she was pleading with him and she looked upset. She must have been upset because otherwise she would have seen me. And then . . . I couldn't help noticing . . . she wrote him a cheque. Ah . . .!' She gave a little start.

'You've remembered something else?'

But she wasn't listening to him. Her accustomed ear had caught the sound of the lift doors closing out on the landing.

'It's my son. I can put the rice in.'

When the Marshal got back to his Station young Brigadier Lorenzini was in the duty room.

'Everything all right?'

'All under control, Marshal. The boys are upstairs cooking their supper. I'll go off duty when they've finished.'

'You can go off now. You've done far more than your share of hours today.'

Lorenzini didn't wait to be asked twice but reached for his greatcoat. He had only been married and living out of barracks for a few months.

The Marshal's own wife and two little boys were down in Syracuse but they would soon be joining him. As Lorenzini clattered out in a rush he tried to imagine what it would be like to lead a normal family life again, remembering the young student of architecture coming home to a bowl of hot soup in the neat dining-room where the television was already on for him. The Marshal's own quarters were in darkness. Instead of going there he went upstairs to see how the lads were faring.

They, too, had the television on but beside it were two
small closed-circuit sets for keeping a check on the gates
outside. The room was steamy.

'What are you cooking?'

'Pasta with tomato sauce and hot peppers—Di Nuccio's
speciality.'

'*Buon appetito!*'

'The same to you, Marshal. Good night.'

'Good night.'

It was after nine o'clock. The Marshal sat down in his
office to write the daily orders for tomorrow, hoping that
there would be no unexpected calls on his boys. When two
of them came down to take over in the duty room he went
to his own quarters and switched on the light in the kitchen.
He, too, put on a pan of water and reached into the cupboard
for a jar of his wife's tomato preserve. It was almost eight
hours since he had eaten and the smell of other people's
suppers had sharpened his appetite. Waiting for the water
to boil, his thoughts rambled over the various young people
he had dealt with in one way and another that day. First
the ones out at the villa, one of whom might well have been
the lover of the forty-eight-year-old Hilde Vogel; the boy
who had died of drugs at age eighteen and whose bereaved
parents he had visited briefly that evening; the young man
who had to run the family business while trying to study for
his degree in architecture at night. Lastly, his own lads
cooking their supper upstairs, all of them hundreds of miles
from their own homes and families. It was as if all these
youngsters lived in completely different worlds. Especially
the ones at the villa whose world the Marshal couldn't
comprehend at all.

Well, he had done his best that day, tomorrow was his
day off, and with any luck the Captain would have no
further use for him on the Vogel case which left a dirty
taste in his mouth. He would be glad not to be involved
in it any further. He wasn't to know that very soon
something was to happen which would involve him even

more deeply and cause him about as much distress as
any case had ever done before.

CHAPTER 6

The trouble with Guarnaccia, Captain Maestrangelo was
thinking as his driver struggled through the lunch-time
traffic taking him out to a new industrial suburb, was that
he never actually said anything much. He just seemed to
breathe unease or suspicion. It was true that once he started
like that he would pursue his quarry doggedly until he had
tracked him down, if it took him years. But they hadn't got
years. What they had got was a rather snappish young
Substitute Prosecutor called Bandini in charge of the case
and who had made it clear that he wanted some fast action.
The Captain had never liked him and he certainly wasn't
the sort to appreciate the ponderous Marshal. The car
stopped at a busy crossing to let a horde of youngsters in
black tunics pour across the street on their way home from
some nearby school.

He had been tempted to ring the Marshal that morning
as soon as he had finished reading the report he had sent
over but he had put the receiver down again without asking
for the number. After all, it was his day off. The Captain
was pushing all his men too hard, he knew. In the end, after
comparing Guarnaccia's report with the statements made
by the hotel staff, he had decided to go out by himself.

The car moved off again and joined the queue at the next
traffic lights.

The trouble was that they had a lot of odd facts, none of
which seemed to link up. According to the hotel receptionist,
Hilde Vogel had taken periodic trips abroad. Paris, Vienna
and Brussels were some of the ones he remembered. All the
tenants at the villa were young foreigners, which suggested
that she might have picked them up on these trips, and that

the newspaper adverts, if they existed at all, were a blind. The agent at Greve had been able to tell the local Marshal nothing other than that he received and answered the inquiries that came in and prepared the contracts.

But if she had indeed picked them up like that, would they be paying the high rent? That wasn't fictional, at any rate, the agent had been able to assure them of that.

The car was now travelling along a broad road with new factories on each side interspersed with petrol stations and high rise apartment blocks.

Only two of the facts that had emerged appeared to have something in common. About a month before her death, Hilde Vogel had been seen in a restaurant with a tall young man, and at about that period a tall man had visited her at the Riverside Hotel. These facts didn't coincide with the murder but at least they seemed to coincide with each other.

'Left here, I think,' the driver said suddenly, interrupting the Captain's thoughts. 'Ugly area, this.'

The car pulled up outside a block of flats identical to all the other blocks. It was bright and sunny but a cool wind was blowing scraps of paper along the wide street.

'Wait for me here,' the Captain said, getting out, 'I shouldn't be more than half an hour.'

Going up to the fifth floor in the cramped lift, he wished again that the Marshal were with him. He was better at this sort of thing.

'Signora Querci?'

The young woman who opened the door looked surprised at first but she realized almost immediately what he had come about.

'I expect it's my husband you want to talk to?'

'Yes. I hope he's awake.'

'Come in.' A little girl had appeared and was staring up at the Captain, clutching all the while at her mother's skirts.

'I'm sorry to disturb you at home but it's rather urgent.'

'That's all right; we've just eaten.'

Nevertheless, she took him into the small kitchen where the table had been cleared of plates, and a typewriter set up. The little girl followed them in and climbed on to a stool at the corner of the table where there was an exercise book and some coloured felt tips. The small flat was very warm and a smell of cooking still hung in the air.

'I do a bit of typing for the extra money.' The young woman had a pretty, almost childish face with a pronounced turned-up nose, but her plump figure, too broad in the hips, suggested she was in her mid-thirties. 'My husband will be in shortly. He always goes down to buy cigarettes after lunch and have a coffee in the bar. I never drink it. Please sit down.'

'Thank you.' The little girl continued staring at the Captain, but when he looked at her she ducked her head and began colouring fiercely.

'I'm sure my husband won't be long,' repeated the woman, not knowing what else to say. After a short silence she suddenly seemed to feel she'd been rude and added, 'I'm sorry, I can't even offer you a coffee. My husband always goes to the bar, you see, and I don't . . .'

'Please don't worry. I've already had coffee,' lied the Captain, who hadn't even managed to have lunch. 'Your husband doesn't sleep during the day?'

'Only until lunch-time. Otherwise he'd have no life at all.'

'I understand. It must be difficult for you, too.'

'Difficult? You can't imagine. It's no joke being alone at night in an area like this. I have good neighbours, but even so, after eight years of it I've had enough—'

She stopped suddenly and said to the child, 'Go in the other room and do your homework.'

'I'm doing it here.'

'Do as you're told. Go on.'

The little girl climbed down from her stool and picked up her book and colours, sneaking a last look at the uniformed man as she went out.

'I've worked in a hotel myself,' the woman went on as soon as the door closed. 'In fact, that's how we met, in Milan.' She seemed glad enough to have someone to talk to now that her initial shyness had worn off. 'I was always dog-tired and it's not as though the pay's anything to write home about. If I had my way he'd get out, and I've told him so, but he has no push.'

The Captain remembered Guarnaccia's description of the soft-spoken night porter who seemed contented enough with his lot.

'He's a good husband, don't get me wrong, but hotel work isn't right for him. Then when a nasty business like this happens you're involved whether you had anything to do with it or not. He should have got out before, when we left Milan.'

'I expect it's difficult to find anything else.'

'Not at all, that's just the point! You see, my father has a business, a grocer's shop in the centre—I was born and brought up here—and he'd gladly sell it to us on instalments. It's more than time he retired. But with men pride always comes first, even before the good of the family, and Mario won't hear of it until he can get together the sort of deposit that my father could get from anyone else. Well, you can imagine trying to save anything on a night porter's salary! I've been on at him for years but he won't budge—Hush! That's him now.'

As the front door closed quietly they heard the little girl's voice: 'There's a carabiniere! Can I come in the kitchen with you?'

'No. Get on with your homework, there's a good girl.'

'You said you'd help me. You promised.'

'I will, in just a minute. Off you go.'

The kitchen door opened. Mario Querci looked different, younger, in the jeans and anorak he was wearing. The Captain had only seen him in the black suit he wore on duty at the Riverside.

'I'm sorry to disturb you at home,' began the Captain.

'That's all right. I suppose it's about Signora Vogel again—don't get up, I'll sit here.'

The kitchen was overcrowded with three adults in it. A quarrel could be heard going on in the flat next door.

'I told the Marshal everything I knew,' Querci said.

'Yes, I realize that. In fact, it's about something I read in your statement that I wanted to ask you. You said a man had been to see Hilde Vogel one night about a month before.'

'That's right. But I said at the time I couldn't remember the exact date and I've no way of checking since he wasn't a guest.'

'I understand that. What would be helpful would be a clearer description of the man.'

'I see. The trouble is, so many people come and go . . .'

'The thing that interests me is his age.'

'Well . . . I'm no hand at judging people's ages, but I'd say he was fiftyish.'

'Fiftyish . . .'

The Captain's disappointment must have shown on his face because Querci went on: 'I told you I'm no judge. I could be wrong by five years either way.'

But not by thirty years! So they were back where they started with a lot of unrelated facts.

'His hair was grey, I'm pretty sure of that,' went on Querci, still trying to be helpful.

'I see. Well, thank you. I apologize again for having disturbed you.' The Captain stood up.

It was Signora Querci who showed him out. From the tiny entrance hall he caught a glimpse of what should have been the living-room. There was a three-piece suite there but the two armchairs had been stacked, one upside down on the other, and the room had been made into a bedroom for the little girl who was lying there on a folding bed with her book and colours.

At the door, Signora Querci glanced back over her shoulder as if she would have liked to say something to him privately, but the flat was so small you could hear every word. In the end she came out on the landing.

'I just wanted to say . . . you won't involve him any more than you have to? In spite of what I said, he's a good man. It's just that he's unlucky.' She seemed genuinely distressed, perhaps a little ashamed of herself. 'I shouldn't have spoken as I did, but there are times . . . cooped up here all day. I hope you understand.'

'Signora, please don't worry about it. It sometimes helps to unburden yourself to an outsider.'

'That's it exactly; To an outsider you can say things you wouldn't normally say.'

But not, thought the Captain, going back down in the lift, in this job. He was tempted to stop off for a moment at Pitti—just to keep Guarnaccia up to date—but again he reminded himself that it was the Marshal's day off and that he no doubt had his own problems to worry about.

'No, no! You're not following me—don't keep interrupting.'

'I'm not interrupting. All I asked was if you could hear me!'

'Don't shout. Of course I can hear you.'

But the Marshal's wife was never convinced, even though she could hear him perfectly well. To make matters worse, the line kept fading for a few seconds every so often, so that he would miss something she said, causing her to shout even more. He was growing a bit red in the face.

'What I'm trying to say is that the boys need the space more than we do. I'm not talking about moving the beds round in their room but giving them our room which is bigger—after all, where are they going to study? We can manage with less space.'

'I don't see why you can't wait till we get up there to decide. Salva? Can you hear me?'

'Because it'll be chaos. I'm trying to get things sorted out.'

'I'd rather you waited. In any case, why can't they study

in the kitchen like they've always done, where I can keep my eye on them?'

'With the television there?'

'We'll move the television. There's the lounge.'

'There's no need to shout, I can—'

'Just wait till I get there. I'll sort it out. You keep phoning up and it's costing a fortune. You know when we got the telephone put in we agreed to phone once a week as usual.'

In fact, she had phoned him just as often, each time with some new problem they hadn't thought about.

'In that case, leave the boys with my sister, like we suggested before and you come up first and see to things.'

'I was the one who suggested it and you said no!'

'Well, now I'm saying yes. After all, if you won't let me do anything . . .'

'All right. I'll speak to Nunziata and see if she's still willing. Have you been busy?'

'Fairly. The usual drug problems.' He had no desire to talk about the Vogel case which he hoped he'd finished with.

'Oh dear, Salva . . . I'm beginning to worry about the boys. After all, they're growing up. You don't get that sort of thing going on here, not like in Florence.'

'We can't change our minds now. You know I could have been waiting years for a posting down there.'

'I suppose so . . .'

'Don't start worrying. They'll be all right.'

But he spent the rest of the night worrying about it himself, and hardly got any sleep at all. Every time he drifted into a doze he would have the same dream of trying to comfort the parents of the drug death boy only to realize that it was his own children they were weeping over and that their son was there with them. Then he would go searching for his two boys all over Florence until he remembered they were still in Syracuse. He was only too relieved to find himself properly awake well before the alarm went off; nevertheless, he felt heavy and depressed all morning and the three hours he was obliged to spend on tedious paperwork did nothing to distract him. When a distraction did arrive he had just settled into his armchair for a rest after lunch. And that wasn't the only reason why it was an unwelcome one.

'I've got Captain Maestrangelo on the line for you, Marshal.'

If it was that wretched Vogel woman . . .

'Put him through—No, wait, I'll come to my office.' So much for his nap. 'Captain?'

'I need your help on the Vogel case.'

'I see. Has something happened?'

'Yes, something has. This morning the Substitute gave permission for the seals to be removed from her room. The manager had been making a fuss and there seemed no good reason to refuse. The seals were removed immediately before lunch and after lunch the chambermaid went up to get the room ready for the next occupant. I won't go into all the details which you'll hear when you get there. The point is that somebody's been into that room and searched it. I want to know who and why.'

'I'd go there myself,' he went on, 'but I've got four men out tailing a smalltime pusher we haven't seen around before, a Moroccan. I think we're finally getting somewhere and I want to be in constant radio contact with them.'

It was only partly true. This drug case wasn't just taking up a lot of his time but all his mental energy, too, which made it difficult to concentrate on anything else. And he was also convinced that Guarnaccia was the one person capable of sniffing out the truth about the Vogel woman.

The Marshal himself had no such conviction. He put down the receiver and began struggling grumpily into his holster. The worst of it was that the protagonist of this episode was sure to be that wretched little chambermaid who only read the horoscopes and who thought nothing of telling him to mind his own business.

'Lorenzini!' He stuck his head round the duty room door.

'Marshal? Is something wrong?'

'No . . . no. Everything under control?'

'Fairly quiet. The patrol car's just been called up to Forte di Belvedere. The residents are complaining about a funny smell.'

'They should have called the *vigili*.'

'They did. It was the *vigili* who called us.'

'Hmph. Well, I don't see why . . . What sort of funny smell?'

'Di Nuccio said cheese . . .'

'*Cheese*? That's all we need.' He was fishing for his dark glasses in one pocket after another. 'I'm going out.'

Perhaps it was just to avoid the chambermaid's confusing and irritating him right from the start that he decided to talk first with the manager, who was hovering anxiously in the reception area when he walked into the Riverside Hotel.

'Please come this way.'

'I'd rather talk here, if it's all the same to you.' The Marshal had an undefined feeling that the reception hall was the key to this whole business if he could only work out how.

It was obvious that it wasn't all the same to the manager who would have much preferred to keep the uniformed intruder out of sight of his guests, but he could hardly say so. The Marshal walked round and lifted the wooden flap to go behind the desk. There he sat himself down heavily on the receptionist's stool and stared about him in silence. Someone had almost certainly managed to leave this hotel with a body dressed in nothing but a fur coat. From where he was sitting he could see straight into the breakfast lounge which wasn't partitioned off. A little to the left was the lift, which had a glass panel in the door, and next to that the service lift and the wide, blue-carpeted staircase. To his right were the revolving doors of the only exit. A group of four middle-aged tourists got out of the lift and went out, laden with guidebooks and cameras.

'Where's the receptionist?' he asked after a moment.

'In my office waiting for you with the chambermaid and the cleaner. I've been keeping an eye on things here. I presumed you'd want to speak to them.'

'Yes.' But he didn't move. His big eyes went on moving slowly over everything in his view. The idea of anyone trying to go through the revolving doors with that cumbersome burden and at the risk of bumping into someone immediately outside was absurd. The lift, then. Straight down to the garage to a waiting car? But he could see into both lifts quite easily and the noise of one of them going down would be heard clearly in the early hours of the morning when the hotel was silent. Mario Querci, the night porter, insisted that he had seen and heard nothing though he had been sitting right here.

'Where does he go,' said the Marshal, almost to himself, 'to relieve himself?'

'I beg your pardon?'

'The night porter. He can't sit here all night without going to relieve himself. Where does he go?'

'I see. Behind you, in the same corridor as my room and the accounts office. There's a staff toilet between the two.'

'Hmph.' Even so, nobody waiting upstairs for the chance to get out with the body could have had any way of knowing . . .

After waiting with obvious impatience for a few more moments the manager said tersely, 'I don't quite see what that has to do with—'

'What?' The Marshal interrupted him, coming to himself quite suddenly.

'I was going to say that your question doesn't seem to have much to do with what's just happened.'

At least they might send somebody a bit brighter to deal with things!

'No . . .' the Marshal admitted slowly, 'probably not . . .'

For the first time he looked carefully at the manager who had remained on the other side of the desk and was looking decidedly agitated. He was a big, imposing man with iron grey hair and piercing eyes.

'You're from the north . . .?' It was more of an observation than a question.

'From Milan.'

'That's right . . . Captain Maestrangelo mentioned it . . . And the owner of this place—'

'Is also Milanese. He has another hotel up there. Would you like to come through to my office or are you intending to question my staff here? I must point out that in consideration for my guests—'

'That's all right,' said the Marshal equably. 'That's all right. I'll talk to them in your office if that's what you prefer. By the way, what happened to the dog?'

'The dog? Ah, Signora Vogel's dog. We had it put down.'

The animated conversation that was in full swing when the manager opened his office door ceased abruptly at the sight of the bulky uniformed figure behind him.

'I'll talk to the chambermaid first,' the Marshal said with an almost audible sigh. He waited until the door closed behind the others before sitting down heavily in the manager's revolving chair and fixing the girl with a stare that dared her to start giving him any cheek. As it turned out, he needn't have bothered. She was a puny creature with a thin colourless face and she kept nervously twisting up strands of limp black hair that had escaped from an elastic band.

'Gave you a fright, did it?' the Marshal asked after observing her for a few seconds.

'I should think it did. Gino said I could easily have been attacked, even killed.'

'Gino said that, did he? But you didn't see whoever it was?'

'No.'

'Then I don't think you need worry. Tell me what happened from the beginning and don't leave anything out, even unimportant things.'

'Well, somebody came this morning—just before lunch, it was—to tell the manager he could use the Vogel woman's room again. There were two men and they took the seals off the room.'

'Do you know what time exactly?'

'Not exactly but it was going on for twelve o'clock because they were still up there when I went to the kitchen for some lunch.'

'Did you eat with your friend Gino?'

'No, he has to eat at eleven because he waits at table. Afterwards I went out and had a coffee.'

'Who with?'

'With my mum. She's a school attendant just near here and we always go for a coffee together when she comes out.'

'Always in the same place?'

'Nearly always. It's the only place round here where tourists don't go and where you don't have to pay extra if you sit down.'

'And did you tell your mother about the seals being taken off the room?'

'Of course I did. Nobody said I shouldn't!'

'All right, all right. Did you tell anyone else?'

'I didn't see anybody else. Everybody in this place knew. They were cracking jokes about there being a curse on the room. The manager got annoyed. I suppose he was scared of the guests hearing something.'

'What happened when you got back to work?'

'The manager told me to get the room ready and I went to the linen store to get sheets and towels.'

'Was there anybody in the bedroom when you arrived?'

'No—I mean yes. I didn't see anybody, but even so . . .'

'Describe what happened when you went in.'

'I went straight through the sitting-room to the bedroom and laid the sheets and stuff on the bed. That's when I noticed that one of the dressing-table drawers was slightly open. I called out to Dina who was in the bathroom—I mean I thought that's who it was. Just imagine if I'd gone in there and—'

'Why did you think the cleaner was there?'

'I heard her. At least, I heard a noise of somebody moving in there and her bucket was propping the bathroom door open.'

'What did you call out?'

'I can't remember . . . something about her playing at carabinieri . . .' The girl reddened. 'I thought she'd been looking through the Vogel woman's room because of the drawer . . .'

'I see. And nobody answered, I take it?'

'I didn't wait for an answer. I'd started to put a pillow case on and I noticed one of the seams was split. I went off to get another one. That's when I met Dina. She was coming out of the store where they keep soap and stuff, with a bottle of alcohol in her hand.'

'Where is this store room?'

'On the fifth floor, next to the linen store.'

'And Signora Vogel's room is on the third, is that right?'

'Yes, so it couldn't have been Dina who was in there, could it? I told her I'd heard somebody and she said we should call the manager.'

'You didn't go straight back to the room to check if there was anybody still there?'

'Not likely! We sent for the manager and he went. Gino says I did right. He says—'

'Never mind Gino for the moment.' They had certainly given the intruder plenty of time to get away, but he could hardly blame them. 'Are you sure nothing else had been touched in the room except the dressing-table drawer?'

'The manager said after that the wardrobe door was slightly open, too, but I didn't notice it.'

'All right. You can go. Send me the cleaner.'

The cleaner, a plump woman in her fifties, confirmed everything the chambermaid had said and declared stoutly that she had nothing to add. The Marshal took almost half an hour getting her to admit that the five minutes she claimed to have been away from the room to fetch the alcohol were really more like fifteen. She had managed to get in a quick coffee with some crony of hers down in the kitchen before going up to the fifth-floor store room. With the receptionist it was the same story as the night of the murder. He had been at his post the whole time and had seen nobody come past to the stairs or lift.

'Not a soul. At that time, those guests who have lunch here are in the dining-room. Those who eat out at midday either don't come in until evening or they come back for a rest in the afternoon but not as early as that. It's my quietest time of day.'

'What time do you eat?'

'At twelve. The manager takes over here as a rule. He never eats until two-thirty when the guests have finished.'

'Did you talk to any of the guests about this business of the seals?'

'Absolutely not. The manager forbade us to talk about it. That dreadful woman's brought us enough trouble already, without—'

'Were you alone at your desk the whole time?'

'Of course.'

'You're quite sure you weren't distracted, chatting to anyone?'

'No! That is, Querci, the night porter, called in to collect his shoes but I promise you he wasn't talking to me for more than one minute.'

'Why, don't you like him?'

'He's all right. Quiet, keeps himself to himself. I can't say I've anything against him.'

A rarity, the Marshal thought.

'Does he often call in in the afternoon?'

'No, only very occasionally. But he had to collect his shoes, the ones we wear indoors here, and take them to the mender's. He'd forgotten them in the morning when he went off.'

'He changes his shoes to go home?'

'We all do. Rule of the house. We have special light shoes that we work in.'

'And how can you be sure nobody walked in here while you were talking to him?'

'I'm willing to swear on the Bible! He took his shoes and went. *Nobody* could have walked past here without my noticing.'

'Except other members of staff.'

'I don't follow you.'

'You wouldn't take any notice of some member of the hotel staff walking past you.'

'I suppose not . . . but that's not what you asked me.'

'I asked you if anybody walked past to the stairs or lift. What about the manager, for instance?'

'Well, if you put it like that . . . he may have done . . .'

'Where was he, for instance, when the chambermaid and the cleaner sent for him?'

'He was just coming out of the lift. I called to him . . .'

'Exactly.' The Marshal stared at him and shook his head.

'Listen . . . I won't be expected to appear in court over this business, I hope. I did my best to answer your questions but you confused me!'

The Marshal glowered at him. 'You can go. Tell the manager I'm using his telephone and I don't want to be disturbed.'

He dialled a number, muttering to himself.

'Captain? Guarnaccia speaking . . . Yes, I've just finished. No, nothing concrete, but there are some things that want looking into. I don't know if you've finished checking on the backgrounds of the staff here . . . No, I wasn't thinking of anything as definite as previous convictions but I think a call to our people in Milan might be a good idea . . . The other hotel, yes. When you've got some information we can make a move. Nevertheless . . . there's a lot missing. We know too little about the woman and what she was up to—and I'm still not happy about the goings-on at that villa. All those youngsters . . . Anyway, I'll send you my report—What? The Substitute Prosecutor? I don't know what you can tell him that's definite. Wait . . . Tell him we need the room sealed up again, at least until we've heard from Milan. The manager here will be livid but I can't help that. I'll wait here until it's been done so there can be no more funny business. But I hope they won't be long, I want to get back to Pitti.'

When he did get back the two boys on duty were waiting for him anxiously.

'You're wanted up at the Forte di Belvedere, Marshal. Lorenzini's already gone up there. There's been a body found and he thinks it's probably another drug death.'

The Marshal, who had begun to unstrap his holster, buckled it up again and went out without a word.

Lorenzini broke away from the group of people standing by some tangled bushes on the steep narrow lane running up beside the city wall towards the fort.

'I'll go back down if you can take over here.' He was looking a little green

'Is it a drug death?'

'Probably. This is a popular spot for a fix. The doctor's taking a look now.'

'All right, you can go.'

The doctor was coming out from behind the bushes when the Marshal joined the group. People were looking out of their windows in the houses on the left side of the lane. The photographer must have already left but the *vigile* was still there with a magistrate whom the Marshal didn't know. The *vigile* was only young and he looked as green as Lorenzini had looked. The smell coming from the bushes was very strong and undoubtedly cheesy. An ambulance was waiting a little higher up the lane. The Marshal waited, impassive behind his dark glasses, while the doctor talked to the magistrate.

'It's a pity the whole body wasn't immersed in the ditch. With the head being out of the water the rats have left you nothing to identify. As you can judge by the smell, the corpse is saponified so it's been in that wet, warm spot for at least forty days or so, probably more like two months. I'd say it was a youngster but I'm going by the clothes more than anything. If you want to remove him . . .'

The magistrate nodded to the two porters who were waiting at a distance, smoking. The Marshal, still silent, followed them behind the bushes and looked down into the ditch where the soles of a pair of gym shoes were the first thing he saw in the water. The spring was bubbling gently past the body, carrying dead leaves and scraps of rubbish with it.

For all the care they took in moving the corpse which was heavy with absorbed water, the light, skeletal head broke away and had to be taken separately. One of the yellow, waxy hands had a sort of bracelet on it made of plaited leather.

The *vigile* switched on his radio and began talking into it. The ambulance moved off. Some of the watching neighbours closed their windows.

And still the Marshal hadn't said a word.

CHAPTER 7

'We think he suspects he's being followed!'

'We're sure he does . . .'

'Even so, we kept on his tail and when he met up with the other two—'

'Wait! Before that, he went in a bar and that's where I managed to get close up—'

'One at a time,' the Captain suggested. His four plainclothes boys had erupted into his office at six in the evening and piled their radios on to his desk, all of them breathless and wanting to speak at once so that he constantly had to interrupt them.

'Where did he meet up with the other two?'

'On the other side of the Ponte Vecchio, under the tunnel.'

'You could recognize them again?'

'Easily! Especially the girl, she had a pair of . . . excuse me, sir—but she had a really low-cut sweater on.'

These boys had only been with the Captain a few months. They were bursting with enthusiasm and had the energy and stamina that this sort of work required. But they were so young and had no experience. It was always the same problem. Men with the amount of experience desirable didn't have that tireless energy and couldn't blend in with gangs of drug addicts the way these could.

'Why do you think he suspects he's being followed?'

'Because when the three of them met up and set off towards the station they walked in Indian file a long distance apart.'

He knew all right, in that case. But probably because he'd heard something. It was unlikely that he'd distinguished the four boys who looked for all the world like a seedy bunch of bag snatchers on the lookout for the tourist's handbag that would buy them their next fix.

'Did you manage to get anything to eat?'

'Not till three this afternoon! And then it was only a sandwich. You can bet he didn't have breakfast at seven like we did!'

'Go and eat now, in that case, and then come back here. I want to brief you for tomorrow.'

'Are we to go on following him?'

'No. I doubt if he's recognized you, but if he suspects he's being followed he's not going to be seen with the dealer and that's the man we want. We'll leave him alone for a few days and work on the informers. I'm putting you four on another case.'

Seeing their enthusiasm evaporate and their faces downcast as if he were punishing them, he added, 'You did a good job and if I risk his spotting you I'll have to take you off the case for good. As it is, I'm transferring you to the Vogel case for two or three days.'

'That foreigner in a fur coat job?'

Their disappointment remained evident. As they went out one of them turned to say, 'We heard another boy was found dead yesterday up near the fort. Do you think it's another bad dose death to do with this case?'

It wasn't going to be easy transferring their attention.

'No,' the Captain said. 'Judging from the doctor's preliminary findings, it happened too long ago. Hurry up and get something to eat.'

When they had gone he picked up the telephone receiver. 'Get me Marshal Guarnaccia at Stazione Pitti.'

The first thing the Marshal said was, 'Have you had my report?'

'I've got it here now. It sounds as if it will turn out to be another drug death but probably from an overdose, nothing to do with the case we have on hand since it happened some time ago, according to the doctor.'

'Yes, some time ago . . .'

'He wouldn't have been up there giving himself a fix on his own, and since he had no documents on him it's likely that his friends got rid of them before abandoning him so as not to be picked up as witnesses.'

'I expect so.'

'Well, we'll see what the autopsy can tell us. I phoned you to give you the latest information on the Vogel case. The lawyer called me back. Her bank in Florence was Steinhauslin. She had a foreign account there and sent cheques once a month to a bank in Mainz in West Germany to an account in the name of H. Vogel.'

'She sent money to herself?'

'It certainly sounds like it. What's more, incoming cheques apart from the rent of the villa were always from a bank in Geneva and were definitely transfers from her own account there.'

'Hmph . . .' The Marshal, who had never had any money other than his army pay, made nothing of that.

'I've informed the Substitute Prosecutor and now we're waiting to see if the lawyer comes up with anything useful from the German end. We need more personal background on the woman. As far as finding witnesses is concerned, we've come to a dead end. Nobody saw the body being dumped in the river.'

'It couldn't have happened further upstream where there are no houses?'

'No. Judging by the time of death and the sluggishness of the river, which was very low, she was almost certainly dumped from one of the city centre bridges, probably the one nearest the hotel.'

'I see.'

'There are alternative theories but none of them can really be considered feasible. If she was killed in a car in some deserted lovers' lane it would have to have happened a few hours' drive out of Florence to account for the amount of time she was lying in one position after death. Nobody would risk driving all that way with a corpse in his car to then try and get rid of it in the city centre when he could have dumped it in the nearest ditch.'

'No . . .'

'It seems certain she was killed in her own bedroom and kept there until the early hours of the morning when there was little risk of anyone seeing the body being removed.

'Yes . . . though somebody might have wanted us to think so . . .'

'It could hardly have been worth the risk.'

'I suppose not . . . I was thinking of that villa, and the boy in the restaurant.'

'None of that need have had anything to do with the murder.'

'No. Did you get anything from Milan?'

'Something and nothing. There was an incident, at the other hotel belonging to the same owner, as you suggested.

But nothing came of it. In fact, our people had difficulty tracking it down because no official complaint was made. In the end they got the information from a retired waiter there. I'll send you the details. Strictly speaking, it doesn't bear directly on this case, it can't be called evidence.'

'Have you decided what to do?'

'The Substitute Prosecutor will give the order for the seals to be removed tomorrow evening. Whoever broke in was disturbed last time and probably didn't get what he wanted. I may be wrong, of course, but it's worth trying. If he turns up again we'll be waiting for him.'

'I see.' The Marshal coughed and waited.

'Is there something the matter?'

The Marshal coughed again before saying slowly, 'That boy . . .'

'The one in the restaurant?'

'No, no . . . The one we found yesterday.'

It was only then the Captain realized that the Marshal had been listening to him dutifully. If he had come out with it as the boys had done, 'that foreigner in a fur coat job', it couldn't have been any clearer. Orders might be orders and always obeyed, but that wasn't the way to get the best out of people on a job like this. Only yesterday morning he had felt that Guarnaccia was beginning to move in his slow, inexorable way towards whoever had killed Hilde Vogel. Now, because of a dead drug addict he had lost him. He was on his own again. Nevertheless, all he said was, 'Do you think you know who he is?'

'No. I've no idea . . . it's not that. But the doctor said he may have been dead two months.'

'So I understood.'

'And that he was probably very young, adolescent.'

'It's more than likely.'

'Two months . . . and nobody . . . He must have parents somewhere.'

'There was an article in the paper this morning, that may produce something, though you remember that in the case of the Vogel woman it didn't do much good.'

But the Marshal was not to be distracted.

'This is a youngster, practically a child. Why has nobody come looking for him in two months? Where's his mother?'

'Remember that a lot of the young addicts hanging around Florence are not from here, and they're not the sort to write to their parents every week. No doubt they've no idea where he's been for some time and wouldn't suspect that anything might have happened to him.'

When the Marshal didn't answer he said, 'Are you still there? He could be a foreigner, you know. Remember those kids out at the villa . . .'

But the Marshal didn't take the bait. 'I'll start checking with the consulates,' he said. 'First thing tomorrow.'

The Captain gave it up and rang off.

The Marshal was as good as his word and the pale sun had barely appeared over the rooftops next day when he set out in his own little Fiat. It was the busiest time of the morning when people were hurrying to work and groups of children blocked the narrow pavements, chattering and screeching until the first bell went when they would make a dash for the inner courtyard of their schools. Although it was still quite warm during the day there was a chilly mist about at this hour and most people were wearing their green lodens. There were fewer tourists in the streets at last, the cafés had taken in their tables and the movement was faster and noisier now that the Florentines had returned to take over their city.

There was something, the Marshal thought, as crowds of youngsters on mopeds dodged and swerved around his car, that his wife had told him to do that morning. She had rung him yet again the evening before. Whatever it was, it would have to wait. He parked as near as he could manage to the British Consulate, walked back along the swarming embankment and climbed the pale marble stairs to the first floor. He was there for about fifteen

minutes and left, none the wiser, to walk round the corner
to the French consulate on the Via Tornabuoni. Every
visit went more or less the same way. The first thing they
did was to take him to the notice-board where photographs
of missing persons thought to be in Florence were posted.
Each time he would have to explain that a photograph
was no help to him, that the boy no longer had a face.
The height, hair colour and age might help. He was
shown two boys who had vanished three years before at
age sixteen. One had black hair and the other red. What
had they been doing on holiday without their families at
that age? There was a husband who had gone missing
from a coach tour. His wife had sent over a picture of
him sitting in a deck chair in their small suburban garden.
The morning wore on and the Marshal, plodding through
the streets in the mild sunshine, began to wonder if it were
the same everywhere or if it were only Italy that attracted
fugitives from the rest of Europe.

At one o'clock he got back into his car, slammed the door
three times because it never would close, and set off back to
his Station in the lunch-time rush hour. He was brooding
and puzzled. When Lorenzini greeted him with, 'Your wife
telephoned . . .' he only mumbled, 'I'll ring her back after
lunch,' and went off to his own quarters to mull things over
in peace.

He emerged two hours later, announced that he was going
out again and drove away, his face heavy and expressionless
behind the dark glasses.

He was gone for a long time. When he came in again he
automatically opened the door of the duty room to see that
everything was all right, but he didn't speak to the two boys,
only looked at them in a blank sort of way and then closed
the door again. In his own office he sat down slowly at his
desk and waited a moment, his big hands on his knees. He
was breathing heavily as though he were distressed. He
looked at his watch which showed five to six. Then he looked
at the telephone and reached out his hand, but instead of

picking up the receiver he switched on the desk lamp because the light was already fading.

After sitting there a little longer he mumbled to himself, 'I don't know . . .' and gave a little snort.

For a long time he stared with his big, slightly bulging eyes at the wall opposite where a map of the city centre showed his Quarter outlined in red.

When Lorenzini looked in on him half an hour later he was laboriously filling in the daily orders for tomorrow and he looked to be in a bad temper.

The Captain was debating with himself whether to go to bed. He'd had little enough sleep that week and since it was only ten o'clock in the evening nothing was likely to happen for at least two or three hours, if anything happened at all. Two of his plainclothes boys, suitably cleaned up and smartly dressed, were installed in the Riverside Hotel on the third floor. Nobody knew them since they hadn't been on this case until now. All the job needed was the ability to stay awake and listen. If he turned up they would have no difficulty catching him. All the Captain had to do was wait, and there was nothing to prevent him getting some sleep in the meantime. Probably he would have done so if it hadn't been for having that impatient young Substitutue Prosecutor on his back night and day. Maestrangelo was accustomed to waiting patiently and he trusted his boys, but being constantly under outside pressure made him nervous. If he went to bed he wouldn't sleep. The Substitute had even tried to insist that this operation should take place the night before.

'I don't see any good reason for losing another day. This case is dragging on too long as it is and I must say that your present line of inquiry hasn't produced much.'

The Captain could hardly point out that the line of inquiry was that ordered by the Substitute himself, who was far too occupied with a more newsworthy trial in the assize courts to give much attention to this case. He did explain patiently that there hadn't been a room available on that floor until today and that, even if there had been, it would have looked pretty odd to apply and remove the seals in one day without even giving the manager time to have his lawyer ring the Procura to complain.

'Well, I hope something comes of it,' was the Substitute's parting shot.

And if nothing did?

Well, they would get there in the end, it would just take longer and the Substitute would become even more of a pain in the neck than he was being already.

The Captain decided not to go to bed. He filled in a couple of hours with paperwork which he would have no time for tomorrow if this operation turned out to be successful.

After that he got up to stretch his legs and looked out of his window at the lighted street below. A stream of squad cars was leaving the building as the midnight shift of the *Radiomobile* went on duty. There was still plenty of traffic on the roads but few pedestrians. A small group of people came to a halt directly under the window and stopped to argue about something before disappearing into the main entrance, no doubt to register some complaint. Any time now something might happen at the Riverside. Whatever the intruder had been looking for the other day must have been pretty incriminating to warrant such a risk. And he must have known for sure that it hadn't already been found by the Captain's men since otherwise he would have been questioned about it, even arrested. What he didn't know, the Captain was convinced, was where it was hidden. If he had known that he wouldn't have opened both the dressing-table drawer and the wardrobe.

As he sat down again at his desk the telephone rang.

'Yes?'

'Marshal Guarnaccia for you, Captain.'

'Put him through.' What could he want at this hour?

Surely not another drug death?

'Captain?'

'Speaking.'

'They told me you were still in your office, otherwise I'd
have left you a message for tomorrow.'

'Something's happened?'

'No, no, nothing . . . Have you got somebody with you?'

'No, nobody.'

'I see. Even so, I suppose it could wait until tomorrow. I
imagine you must be busy or you wouldn't be in your office
at this hour . . .'

When the Captain explained to him what was going on,
he said: 'In that case I'll come over right away if you don't
mind. It's about the Vogel case . . .' And with a cough and
an incomprehensible mumble he rang off.

Bemused, the Captain got up again and stood by the
window. He'd been mistaken, then. Yet he could have sworn
Guarnaccia had gone off on some scent of his own and had
abandoned the Vogel case. If that were so, then something
had caused him to change direction again. Perhaps the dead
boy's parents had turned up after all. Well, he would soon
know. The Marshal's little white Fiat came chugging along
Borgo Ognissanti and turned in at the gates. The Captain
sat down to wait.

The trouble was that once Guarnaccia had lumbered in
and sat himself down on the other side of the desk he
evidently didn't know where to begin.

'I don't know where to begin, to tell the truth . . .' The
Marshal stared fixedly at his knees.

'Begin at the beginning,' the Captain suggested, wondering what on earth he was going to come out with that could
be so complicated as all that.

'It's difficult to explain exactly . . .'

Because for the Marshal there was no beginning. There
were just people, and a certain number of images fixed in
his mind. A pair of gym shoes sticking up in a ditch with
the water bubbling around them carrying fallen leaves away;

the musty, neglected villa; all those photographs of missing youngsters pinned on the consulate notice-boards; and the nice woman in the tidy flat getting on with her cooking as she said, 'Perhaps because I've got a son that age myself . . .'

And, if the truth were told, what was preying on his mind most of all was that an hour ago he had suddenly remembered what it was his wife had asked him to do that morning. He should have gone across to the Middle School in Piazza Pitti and registered his two boys there. Instead of which he had not only forgotten to do it but had spent the entire day inwardly fulminating against neglectful parents. It was that which, in the end, had made him decide to ring the Captain. He was so full or remorse at his own stupidity that he needed the Captain's confirmation that what he had been doing all day was important. Otherwise he would have waited until he could arrange all his feelings and suspicions into some semblance of logical order.

Now he was sitting there with a jumble of pictures in his head and the Captain waiting patiently in front of him. With an effort of will he raised his eyes to fix them on his superior officer and started his story in the middle.

'This afternoon I went to the Medico-Legal Institute.'

When the Captain made no response but only looked at him inquiringly he carried on, sometimes letting his big eyes rove over the spacious office, sometimes staring down at his knees, and every now and then watching the Captain's face and wondering what sort of impression he was making, if any.

After all, there was nothing you could call concrete. He had set out for the Medico-Legal Institute with no clear idea in mind. He just felt the need to see the faceless boy again, get closer to him. Even so, when the idea did form itself, it seemed as if it had been there all along.

Professor Forli was always a willing talker and, though he hadn't yet begun work on the autopsy, he accompanied the Marshal himself. They had faced each other over the body that lay in its cold storage drawer.

'We store dismembered parts separately,' Forli had explained as he pulled the drawer out. 'But since there's practically nothing to see from the shoulders up I suppose you wouldn't be interested.'

'No, no . . .'

'If the smell's too much for you I can get you a mask.'

The Professor himself was evidently immune to it.

'It doesn't matter,' the Marshal said. He was so preoccupied as to be barely conscious of the bad cheese smell anyway. He stared down intently at what remained of the boy, seeing the tell-tale puncture marks on the greasy yellow arms.

'He's very thin,' he murmured after a moment.

'Most addicts are. Though this one probably hadn't been at it long. There are no scars on the thighs. I'll probably start work on this tomorrow if nothing more urgent crops up in the meantime. The trouble with your saponified corpse is that once it dries out it becomes very fragile, chalky, so the sooner I start the better. Nevertheless, I can tell you now that he'll be a mess inside and there won't be much I can tell you.'

'But if he's so well preserved . . .'

'The process works from the outside in, which is a help in the case of superficial markings like these needle scars but no help at all if you're interested in what he last ate, what state of health he was in, and so on.'

'And the cause of death . . .?'

'Matter of luck.' The Professor shrugged. 'In this case we've got the evidence in front of us that he was an addict. Added to which, the circumstances in which he was found, in an area popular with addicts, and the lack of documents, suggest an overdose. His friends would abandon the body as a matter of course. But I can't prove it for you. There'll be nothing left to analyse of his liver and the blood, too, will have decomposed. There's no flesh left on the neck and face, for instance. What if somebody strangled him like the fur coat woman? It's unlikely, but what I'm saying is I can't prove otherwise.'

'No . . .' Was it then that the idea had suggested itself, or come to the surface of his consciousness as though it had always been there? It wasn't that he thought the boy had been strangled, though that, too, might eventually turn out to be a possibility to explore.

Now he looked at the Captain, watching him carefully as the other waited for him to come to the point. He could still drop the whole thing as being too vague but he went on guardedly.

'The autopsy report on the Vogel woman . . .'

'Yes?'

'You haven't still got a copy?'

'The Substitute has it at the Procura.'

That had been stupid, the Marshal thought. There must have been another copy at the Medico-Legal Institute. It would have been enough to ask the Professor. That way he could have mulled the thing over before sticking his neck out.

'I was wondering,' he said slowly. 'You gave me a summary of it but you didn't mention . . . I wondered if she'd ever had a child.'

'Yes,' the Captain said. 'She did.'

'How long ago? Did it say?'

'If I remember rightly there was a scar mentioned dating back fifteen to twenty years.'

The Marshal relaxed visibly and he no longer minded letting the images tumble out just as they came.

'The thing is that when I talked to the woman who'd seen Signora Vogel in the restaurant with a young man, almost a boy . . . well, what I had at the back of my mind was that if the woman herself was there with her son, what was to stop Signora Vogel being there with *her* son . . . only I didn't know that she had one. And then, that woman wasn't stupid and you can usually tell when you see a mother and son together . . . But you see, Signora Vogel's been living here for fifteen years. What I'm getting at is that if it was her son, then, even so, she hardly knew him. They couldn't have had that sort of relationship . . . I don't know if I'm making any sense at all.'

'Go on.'

'Those boys at the villa . . . I still think you should talk to them. I'm not competent. One might have known her, he wasn't paying rent . . . And then there's another who disappeared shortly after he arrived here. He's supposed to have gone to Greece, but even so . . .'

'You're thinking this dead boy could be one of them? That he may be this woman's son? But she might have had a daughter, for all we know—and this boy you say went off to Greece, he had an English name.'

'That doesn't really prove anything if you'll pardon my saying so. And then there's the other one. We don't know anything about him. He wasn't on your list of tenants or the agent's either. I haven't any real proof, it's just that things started to happen about the time those boys arrived . . .'

That was true. The visit of the grey-haired man, the boy in the restaurant . . .

'But she wasn't killed until a month after that and that boy was already dead then,' the Captain pointed out.

'I could be mistaken,' the Marshal insisted, his face and voice saying the opposite.

'I'll go out and take a look at this villa.'

'With a warrant,' the Marshal added, addressing his knees.

'With a warrant. But I hate to think what the Substitute's going to say—'

The telephone rang.

'Yes?'

'We've got him, sir! But we don't know what to do now. We can't arrest him *in flagrante* because—'

'What's gone wrong? What did he take from the room?'

'That's the trouble, sir, he hasn't taken anything, so—'

'I told you not to disturb him! To wait until he came out!'

'We did wait, sir, but he came out empty-handed. What could we do? We can't arrest him, can we? Not just for being in there. After all . . .'

'No. You can't. Bring him in.'

'Should we—'

'Bring him in!'

The Captain slammed the phone down, his face white, his fingers tapping the desk. For a while he quite forgot the presence of the Marshal, who sat very still and silent. When he got control of his temper again he said shortly:

'They're bringing Querci in.'

'Hmph.'

'If he won't talk I'll arrest him for reticence. If he'd only found what he was looking for in that room!'

'Maybe he—'

'I'll not only arrest him for reticence, he'll get a judicial communication for the murder.'

'It's always possible that . . .'

'I'm going to ring the Substitute now. He's the one who wanted action, so let him get out of his bed and see some!'

The Marshal decided he'd stuck his neck out enough for one day. He got to his feet mumbling something about getting back and the Captain let him go, not without a vague feeling of relief that he wouldn't be around when the Substitute turned up. But he only recognized that little weakness in himself much later when he found time to regret it.

CHAPTER 8

'The incident in Milan. I'd like to hear your side of the story before anything else.'

'I don't suppose you'll believe me. I don't think anybody did, not even my wife, even though the matter was dropped.'

'Presumably the manager believed you.'

'He helped me. He's a distant cousin of my wife's. That's

why she went to work up there. It doesn't mean he believed me. He helped me because of my wife, the family. Otherwise . . .'

'I'd like to hear your side of it, even so,' the Captain persisted gently. His anger had left him the minute the grey-faced night porter had been brought through the door. When they had asked him the formal questions, *Do you intend to answer? Do you intend to tell the truth?* he had only said yes to the first. At the second a few beads of perspiration had appeared on his upper lip.

'It was eight years ago . . . I suppose you already know that.'

'You were the receptionist on day duty then?'

'Yes. The woman . . . had been in the hotel three weeks. She'd been flirting with me all along but only in a bantering sort of way. The usual thing.'

'But then she went further?'

'You understand the sort of woman I mean. Well-off and bored, not as young as she was. A man in uniform who's paid to be at their service . . . for them he's no more than a toy. I don't know if you understand what I mean.'

'I understand.' The Captain had come across one or two of them himself in the course of duty. 'There are some men who aren't averse to taking advantage of a situation like that,' he said.

'I'd been married only a short time and we had just found out my wife was expecting. What's more, she was still working in the hotel.' There was no anger in his mild voice but his face had reddened.

'What happened to precipitate things?'

'She rang for me to go up to her room one evening. I was just about to go off duty. I remember I was to accompany my wife to the doctor's because she'd been feeling a bit off colour. The first few months were difficult for her.'

'And you went to this woman's room?'

'I didn't think anything of it, to tell you the truth. She'd asked me to post a letter for her on my way home. You see,

I was used to her sort of behaviour and I'd never had any real trouble in that line.'

'What did she do when you got there?'

'In the first place she wasn't dressed—I still didn't catch on because it was the time when the guests were getting ready for dinner. She'd just had a shower, she said. She was wearing a bathrobe. She gave me the letter—there really was a letter—and then she asked me to have a drink with her. She kept a bottle of whisky in her room.'

'Did you refuse?'

'Yes, but she took no notice, just went on talking and poured two drinks. She put both of them on her bedside table and lay down. The bathrobe wasn't fastened . . .'

'What did you do?'

'At first I just stood there staring. If I'd thought on before going up there I'd have managed to get out before that, but she caught me unawares and I couldn't do anything but stare. If I'd handled things better, not been so embarrassed, I could have passed the thing off easily enough. If only I'd realized sooner! I wasn't thinking. I was a bit worried about my wife and I just wasn't paying attention. She told me to come and get my drink. I thought I could manage to drink it down in one and get out fast. But when I reached out my hand she took hold of me and made me touch her. That was when . . . she wasn't young, you see. She was a good-looking woman and always well-dressed, but her breast was . . . very soft and limp . . .'

'You were disgusted?'

'No. Not disgusted, honestly not that. Just surprised because I'd only ever known young girls—before I was married, I mean. In any case she must have read the expression on my face and since I stood there without making a move she sat up and started abusing me. I realized when she came closer to my face that she must have had a few drinks before I arrived. She ripped off the bathrobe. *"What's the matter, am I too thin for you? Not as good as your tubby little wife, is that it? Do you know how many men would like the chance you've got—and not men of your class and breed, either!"* All of a sudden she began laughing hysterically. *"So that's what it's come to! Turned down by a creature like you!"*

'She was still almost laughing but she took a vicious swipe at my face. All I did was to try and grab her arm to stop her but she was too fast for me, with the result that I scratched her forearm very slightly and her left breast. I tried to quieten her. After all, the people in the adjoining rooms must have been able to hear her. They did hear her, as it turned out, and the evidence, of course, was all against me. They heard a scuffle and her screaming and when they came to the door to see what was the matter they saw her naked and scratched and crying, pushing me out of the room, and me resisting because I was still hoping to calm her down. I suppose I can't blame anybody for not believing me. I probably wouldn't have believed it myself.'

'She claimed you'd attacked her?'

'Yes. The manager was called immediately. There was a terrible scene.'

'But I understand there was no official complaint made. Our people in Milan have no record of one.'

'Even so, she insisted on calling the carabinieri. By the time they arrived she'd passed out. She must have drunk a lot, I suppose, but I've often thought since that she was playacting and that she'd had second thoughts about telling her story officially, as it were. After all, that would mean I'd have to tell my side of it, with the risk that I might be believed. She left the next day. I think the manager let her off her bill provided she took the matter no further. He also told her I'd be removed from the hotel and I suppose that satisfied her more than anything.'

'And you moved to Florence?'

'The owner of that hotel had just bought the Riverside and was sending the manager down here. I came with him and my wife gave up working since she wasn't too well anyway.'

'They made you night porter, or was it your choice?'

'It was the manager's decision. That's why I'm sure he never believed my story. I have less contact with the guests than I did. I admit that for me it was a relief, even though I was paid less and there was a baby on the way.'

'Nevertheless, you had quite a lot of contact with one guest, it seems.'

'It was what she wanted, and after last time I was afraid . . . Am I going to be arrested?'

'That depends on what you tell me now.'

But the warrant was lying before the Captain on his desk. Needless to say, the Substitute Prosecutor had only stayed just long enough to sign it and had gone off to his bed with barely a glance at Querci. If the latter should be arrested or detained he would return to question him the next day at his convenience.

'Was it the same thing all over again with Signora Vogel?'

'No. It wouldn't be fair to say that. Fair to her, I mean, and now she's dead . . .'

She wasn't just dead, she'd been murdered and thrown in the river.

Must be some sort of loony.

I don't know whether the editor would wear it . . . not if she was just nuts.

That foreigner in a fur coat job.

The only person who showed any delicacy or respect for her was this quiet, frightened man sitting before the Captain with a warrant for his arrest on the desk between them.

'Were you lovers?'

'No. She was an intelligent woman, sensitive too, even though she liked to hide it. It's true that at first I was afraid of another episode like Milan but that wasn't any fault of hers. More than anything, she needed someone to talk to . . . No, not even that because she wasn't much of a talker except on rare occasions.'

'Did she ever talk about her past? When she lived in Germany?'

'Once or twice. I know her father was killed during the war and that although she was very clever at languages she never got a chance to go on with her studies. Instead she went to work in a shop so I suppose they were short of money. Her mother died of some illness not long afterwards. Then I think she married but she never talked about her marriage or about her life after that. Only about her childhood.'

'Did she ever mention a child?'

'No, never. And I had the impression that she either divorced or was widowed quite young. She was always vague about it and I never pressed her. Even so . . . . I told your Marshal that there was certainly a man in her life but I'm sure it couldn't have been her husband.'

'You also mentioned another woman.'

'Yes. But I can't tell you any more than I told the Marshal. It was always just hints here and there. And a lot of what I'm telling you I only guessed or assumed. For instance, I think she must have married somebody fairly wealthy because to live at the Riverside costs money.'

'And her father being killed in the war, was that just guesswork or did she say so?'

'I'm pretty sure she said so.'

'Did she mention a villa to you? A villa near Greve in Chianti?'

'No, never.'

'It was owned by her father and he died only a few years ago.'

'I see.'

He showed no anger even then. There were dark rings under his eyes and it was probable that he hadn't slept properly since the day the Captain had visited his home to ask a question that might well have seemed like a pretext. It wasn't difficult to imagine him lying awake in the mornings in a darkened bedroom with his wife's typewriter clacking in the next room and the neighbours quarrelling beyond the thin walls.

'She may have had her reasons for not telling me about it,' he said gently. 'After all, I never told her about Milan.'

'Nevertheless, if all she wanted was someone to confide in, it seems pointless to have lied to you.'

'Everybody lies, even to the person nearest to them, don't you think? In any case, I don't think it was a question of having someone to confide in. I said before . . . It's not so easy to explain, but I lived alone myself, in Milan, before I got friendly with my wife. It's the little things that make you lonely. Having nobody to grumble to at the end of a bad day, nobody to make you a hot drink when you catch a cold. Whenever she had 'flu or a bad head I would go to the chemist for her, that sort of thing. And there's loneliness for affection, too. I'm not talking about sex, just everyday affection, some sort of physical contact . . .'

'And was there this sort of physical contact between you and Signora Vogel? You said you weren't lovers.'

'I told you, it's not a question of sex. We would talk about it sometimes but that's all. It made for a sort of intimacy that didn't do any harm and over the years we got used to things as they were.'

'In all those years, then, you never touched her?'

'I would massage her neck sometimes if she had a headache. Whether you believe it or not, we were more like brother and sister than anything else. Living alone as she did . . .'

'It was her choice to live alone, presumably.'

'I don't believe so. I'm sure she was disappointed with the way things were, that she had expected something better, maybe from this man I mentioned, but things had dragged on year after year.'

'So you massaged her neck,' the Captain said slowly, 'in the reception hall?'

'What . . .?'

'That's where you told the Marshal your little chats took place. That she slept badly and would come down to talk to you. And you, of course, wouldn't leave your post.'

The atmosphere in the room changed quite suddenly. Until then they might have been having a friendly talk. Now the beads of sweat reappeared on Querci's upper lip but he looked cold. When he didn't answer the Captain continued: 'You went to her room?'

'I . . . I don't remember . . .'

'You went up there on the night she was killed.'

'I didn't see anything, anything at all!'

'You went up there and either you saw what happened or you killed her yourself.'

'No! No, no!'

'Because if someone else did it and you were at your post you had to have seen that somebody not only coming into the hotel but going out with the body.'

'I didn't see anything, I didn't see anything!'

'Everybody lies. You just told me that, didn't you?'

'Yes. But I'm not lying. I didn't see anything. I swear that's the truth, whatever else . . .'

'Whatever else?'

'It's the truth.'

'If you didn't do it, what are you so afraid of? What were you looking for in her room tonight?'

'Nothing.'

'And last time? Were you looking for nothing then, too? It was you who searched the room the other time, wasn't it?'

'I don't . . . I can't remember.'

'What were you looking for tonight?'

'Nothing. I swear it's the truth.'

'I'm going to take that room apart until I find what you were after. If it's there, I'll find it. That can only make things worse for you.'

'I can't help it. I'm telling the truth. I wasn't looking for anything.'

'And you didn't see anything. Who came to see Hilde Vogel the night she died—somebody you know?'

'No.'

'Somebody you don't know? A boy or a man? Which?'

'I didn't see anything! How can I tell you what I didn't see?'

The Captain slammed his hand down on the warrant. 'Do you know what you're doing? If you swear nobody came to see her that night you're leaving yourself as the only suspect!'

'Nobody can prove I killed her when I didn't.'

'No. Nobody could prove you attacked that woman in Milan if you didn't. Did that prevent you losing your job?'

'No.' He was trembling now and his lips were dry and caked.

The Captain rang a bell. 'Bring some water and two glasses.'

As soon as Querci had drunk a little of the water he went on with the questioning even though he had little hope of getting anywhere. If the porter had invented some story, any story, it would have been easy to break him down, but he invented nothing. He went on saying 'I don't know,' 'I don't remember,' 'I didn't see anything.'

After repeating himself and hearing the same answers for a further hour, the Captain decided that a night in the cells might have more effect. Before they took Querci away he asked him, 'Do you want to telephone your wife?'

'Am I under arrest?'

'Yes.'

Querci's face became even more pallid as though he might vomit or even faint, and he wouldn't have been the first to have done so in those circumstances. But all he said was, 'No. She won't be expecting me home until morning, anyway. What's the use of waking her?'

'Take him away.'

The Captain went back to the window and rubbed wearily at his face. It was after three in the morning and the street was silent now in the yellow lamplight. Under one of the lamps a man was hovering, hands deep in his pockets, staring up at the window.

'For God's sake . . .!' He turned and picked up the telephone. 'If that's Galli down there, don't let him come up. Tell him to come back tomorrow.'

'I've already told him, sir.'

'Well, he's still out there. Tell him again. I'm going to bed.'

It wasn't that Guarnaccia ever had much to say for himself but this morning he was singularly silent. He sat beside the Captain in the back of the car with his hands planted on his knees, staring ahead behind his dark glasses. Once they were past the village of Greve he leaned forward slightly every so often to tell the driver which way to turn.

All the way up from Florence the Captain had tried to draw him out on the Mario Querci business but all he said was, 'Have you arrested him?'

'I had no choice.'

'He's not likely to come out with anything to the Substitute Prosecutor this morning?'

'I'm sure he won't.'

After which he had offered nothing more than noncommittal monosyllables and grunts. He seemed satisfied that they were going out to the villa but that was all.

'Left here.'

The car turned on to a lane that wound between vineyards where the harvest had begun and every now and then they passed two lines of men and women snipping at the heavy bunches of grapes while a tractor chugged along at the end of the rows. A white car was coming towards them in the narrow lane and their driver slowed and nosed into a grassy lay-by. The other car drew level and stopped, the driver leaning over to call out.

'Good morning!'

The Captain wound his window down. 'Galli! One of these days you'll really go too far!'

'Couldn't sleep,' said the reporter sheepishly. 'Seriously, if I were in your place I'd arrest that lad Sweeton. He's a born liar.'

'Unfortunately, I can't arrest him for that.'

'Drugs, then. Take my word for it, I know one when I see one. Cocaine. Christ, you could get drunk breathing the air round here.'

Rivulets of wine-coloured water were trickling from a nearby farmhouse into the ditch running along the lane and there was so much fermentation in the air that it really was intoxicating.

'I heard you arrested the night porter.'

'I've no doubt you did. But don't start speculating in print, not now, I'm warning you.'

'Warning taken. Even so, nobody believes he did it, I can tell you that for free. When are you giving us something we can print on this drugs case?'

'When I've got something to give you. Now get out of my way, you're blocking the road.'

'Pleasure. I'm off to bed. But I still think you should arrest that little sod or he'll skip the country.' And Galli drove away, spraying up wine-stained gravel.

The villa looked as deserted as ever when they got there, and the silence was so profound that they could hear in the distance the grape pickers calling for their full baskets to be collected. Nevertheless, this time there was a face at the first-floor window where the shutter was broken, watching their arrival. It had vanished when they got out of the car.

'Wait here,' the Captain told his driver and he approached the front door, the Marshal following behind. The rusted iron bell-pull produced a slow jangling noise. After a few moments a voice from behind the door said, 'You have to come round the back.'

When they got there John Sweeton was waiting in the kitchen doorway. 'The front door doesn't open.' He stood back to let them in. Even before he had spoken the Marshal noticed a difference in his attitude. He was very pale and he watched them nervously as they walked in.

'Just what exactly is going on? I've had a journalist here

pestering me. I warn you now that my father . . .' He tailed off as the Captain stopped and looked him in the face.

'We have a warrant to search this house.'

'Well, if that's all . . .'

'I don't know,' the Captain said quietly, 'whether that's all or not. We'll start with your room if you'd like to lead the way.'

The boy hesitated as though he were going to say something, but he must have thought better of it. He turned and led them out of the sunny kitchen and up the gloomy staircase. Once they were all three in his room he stood still, watching them warily.

'Has your friend Christian come back?' asked the Captain.

'I don't remember saying he was a friend of mine. He was staying here, that's all.'

'Was? I thought he was still staying here?'

'How should I know? His things are still here. His comings and goings are nothing to do with me.' His eyes continually strayed from the Captain to the Marshal, who was moving slowly around the room touching nothing, just looking, his sunglasses dangling from one hand.

'When did you last see him?'

'I can't remember. Some time ago.'

'How long?'

'I don't know.. Why should I—'

'How long? A month? Two months?'

'Something like that. I've forgotten.'

'One month or two?'

'I suppose nearer two.'

The Marshal had come across a copy of the *Nazione* under the bed and was turning its pages slowly. The room smelled strongly of oil paint and turpentine.

The boy had placed himself in front of the easel that stood in the middle of the floor. The landscape was still propped there, the shaft of sunlight from the window falling full on it. The Marshal found the page he was looking for, folded the paper and showed it to the Captain,

who glanced only at the headline before giving it back
without comment.

'You haven't asked us why we're here,' the Captain
observed. 'Aren't you interested?'

'It's nothing to do with me.'

'How can you be so sure of that?'

'Because I haven't done anything.'

'And you don't know anything either, I imagine.'

'That's right.'

The Marshal opened a drawer and shut it again without
looking at the contents. He seemed to be wandering about
the room in an entirely haphazard way. Every time he
passed close to where the Captain and the boy were
standing the latter exhibited a greater nervousness. He
had his hands in his jacket pockets as if to look relaxed, but
the hands were tightly clenched. The Marshal retreated to
one corner of the room, stuffed his glasses into his pocket
and stood watching.

'What have you just taken?' the Captain went on.

'I don't know what you mean.' But the Captain was
staring straight into the tiny pupils of his eyes and the boy
realized it.

'That journalist upset you, did he?'

'He had no right to come prying round here.'

'What did he ask you?'

'There's no reason why I should tell you. Ask him.'

'What did he ask you?' The Captain raised his voice just
a little.

'The same things you're asking—about the woman who
owned this villa.'

'But I haven't asked you anything about the owner of the
villa. I asked you about your friend Christian.'

'He's not my friend!'

'What has he got to do with the owner?'

'Nothing. I don't know.'

'Then why did you think I was interested in the owner
when I asked you about Christian? Marshal!'

Given that the Marshal had stopped looking, he must
have found what he wanted.

Guarnaccia came forward, striding heavily towards the
boy and the easel behind him. The boy started and his hand
shot out of his pocket in an involuntary movement which
knocked a tray of paints and brushes from the easel's ledge
to the floor, scattering tubes and bottles.

'Leave it,' the Marshal said as the boy made to pick
the things up. 'Leave it there, lad, and I'll pick them up
for you.' But he only picked up the paint-stained box
and began examining it carefully. It was divided into
compartments of various sizes. A tiny brown paper package
was stuffed into one of them. The Marshal removed it
carefully and took off the brown paper to reveal a little
polythene bag. It was no more than two inches square
and had been rolled tightly. The Marshal unrolled it,
took a few of the tiny crystals on one fingertip and tasted
them. Then he rolled the bag up again and slipped it
into his top pocket.

'Is there any more of it?' the Captain asked the boy.

'No. I've only ever bought it for my own use and you
can't—'

'All right. You're well-informed about the laws of this
country, I'm sure. But then you read the papers, don't you?
We'll have a look at your friend Christian's room now.'

The boy led the way without a word but they could hear
his shallow, rapid breathing.

The Marshal went straight to the other boy's bedside
table and examined the shrivelled halves of lemon, the belt,
a teaspoon and a cigarette lighter. Then he began searching
the room, this time systematically.

'Whatever Christian did it's nothing to do with me.'

'Then let the Marshal get on with his job and mind your
own business,' the Captain said. 'And meantime, you tell
me just what Christian did. Bear in mind that we know
about him and Signora Vogel.'

'I wasn't involved.'

'Then you've got nothing to worry about. You're just helping us with our inquiries.'

The Marshal was heaving the mattress off the bed. His face was as expressionless as ever but his movements had a ponderous sureness that determined the Captain to take a risk.

'We've found Christian's body,' he said.

The boy swallowed with some difficulty. He didn't speak and his eyes were fixed on the moving bulk of the Marshal who had uncovered two small bags that were taped to the underside of the bed's base. The Captain propelled Sweeton towards the bed and the three of them stood looking in silence, the Marshal puffing a little after his exertions. The air was full of revolving dust.

'We're not going to touch those two packets,' the Captain observed, 'until we get our technicians out here to examine them.'

'What Christian did in here is nothing to do with me.'

'Of course not. I'm interested in what you did in here. No doubt that packet there which is thickly covered in dust contains heroin and has been there since Christian left. But the other one at a guess has been there about half an hour. That journalist did give you a fright, didn't he?'

'It's nothing to do with me.'

'No? But what if that packet contains cocaine. Christian wasn't on cocaine.'

'You can't prove that.'

'Remember we've found his body.'

'You still can't prove it. The paper said that the head was—'

'The paper said? The papers don't know anything about Christian.'

'You two were just looking at the article in my room.'

'The boy we found up near the fort? But the paper didn't say who it was. They don't know. How do you know that was Christian?'

'Because you said so before, that you'd found his body.'

'I didn't say it was that body. I wonder if we'll find your fingerprints on that packet.'

'You won't. And this is not my room. Anything you find in here—'

'That's true. Of course there's nothing to prevent us from finding both those packets in your room.'

'You try anything like that and I'll call my father. I warn you! My father's a judge. You won't get away with anything like that.'

'Your father's not a judge in this country, fortunately for him. I'm afraid he would be embarrassed to have his son in a situation like this if he were.'

'I'm not in any situation. Christian—'

'Christian is dead,' said the Captain quietly, 'and the owner of this villa is dead, and the only person who had any connection with them is you. You are in a situation all right but perhaps you haven't realized yet that we're not talking about drugs but about murder. So it might be as well to call your father anyway.'

If Galli had told him about the arrest of the night porter the Captain would put him inside! But the boy's pale face had reddened in panic and his eyes began darting about the room as if he might make a run for it. The Marshal moved one step closer so that he was practically touching him. Galli hadn't told about the porter.

'I think you'd better come with us,' the Captain went on, 'and we'll talk about it in my office.'

'You can't arrest me without evidence.'

'I'm not arresting you. According to you, only Christian was involved. But Christian's dead and can't tell us about it. Nor can anyone else. If you know anything you'd be well advised to tell us all about it because otherwise we're going to think it was you, aren't we?'

'I'm calling my father.'

'I've already told you that you'd better call your father. You can do that from my office. I'd like to talk to him, too.

I shall need to ask him how much money he's been sending you all year for one thing. Shall we go?'

The boy was put in the back of the car with the Marshal. They travelled along the ochre lanes between vineyards, through the tranquil bustle of the piazza at Greve and down to the city where a snarl of traffic was fighting to get in at the Roman gates. Throughout the journey the boy didn't open his mouth.

When they reached Borgo Ognissanti one of the guards came out to the car to tell the Captain there was someone waiting for him.

'I'm not seeing any journalists.'

'It's a woman, sir.' The guard consulted a slip of paper. 'A Signora Vogel. She's here in the waiting-room if you want her to go up with you.'

CHAPTER 9

'There's somebody with her,' the guard added, 'a lawyer. Do you want me to . . .'

But the Captain had jumped out of the car, waving it on, and was hurrying round to the waiting-room entrance on the right. Unreasonably, he was half expecting to see the thin, blonde woman, to meet that ironic blue-eyed glance. But when he stopped in the entrance he saw a woman of well over sixty years, sitting stiffly on the worn wooden bench with a big, thick-set man beside her. It was the man who got up to introduce himself.

'Captain Maestrangelo? Avvocato Heer. I think we spoke on the telephone. This is Signora Vogel, my client's mother-in-law.'

'We'd better talk in my office.' The Captain led the way along the cloister and up the stairs without further comment. He was trying to decide rapidly whether to make them wait while he went on questioning Sweeton or whether this woman could tell him anything useful that would help him put pressure on the boy. By the time they had reached his office where the Marshal and Sweeton were waiting at the door he had made his decision.

He signed to Guarnaccia to take the boy next door and showed the two visitors inside.

'Please sit down.'

The lawyer spoke to the woman in German and she sat down without answering, holding tightly on to the large handbag placed squarely on her knees. The Captain realized that she was probably much older than he had first thought but the mass of tiny wrinkles covering her whole face was thickly coated with face powder. Her bright little eyes were observing him coldly.

'You are Hilde Vogel's mother-in-law?' he began.

She turned to the lawyer who translated the question for her. She answered him with a one word affirmative.

She maintained this attitude throughout the interview, never troubling again to look the Captain in the face and staring out of the window if he and the lawyer spoke in Italian, as if a foreign language could have no relevance for her. After giving her name as Hannah Kiefer Vogel, and her place of residence as Mainz, she suddenly interrupted and began to speak for herself, pausing occasionally, with evident irritation, to let Avvocato Heer translate.

'I came here as soon as my bank manager informed me about what had happened. I may as well say immediately that my daughter-in-law has caused nothing but trouble in our family since the day my son was foolish enough to marry her. Consequently, the way she died comes as no surprise to me. You will understand when I say that she wasn't our sort, not our sort at all. The Vogel family is much respected in Mainz. Both my husband and my father-in-law were mayors of the city. My own father was a lawyer of some considerable repute. I can safely say that if my husband had been alive my son's marriage would never have taken place. Unfortunately, my husband left his entire estate to our son, giving me nothing more than a moderate income from the capital and the right to reside in the house for my lifetime. The result was that I was obliged to share my home with a shopgirl. Please understand that I am not simply being abusive, this woman worked in a shop owned by a friend of my son's. That was how they met, and in my opinion there was something going on between her and Becker even then. If I tell you that my son hadn't been dead six months when Becker started coming to the house—you can imagine my feelings. I wasn't going to accept that sort of thing under my own roof and I made myself plain on that from the beginning. Nevertheless—'

After listening patiently for some five minutes the Captain made a sign to Heer that he should stop her. If there was anything worse than this woman's vicious respectability it was her assumption that he naturally must agree with her, with her constant 'you will understand'. Besides which, he had no time to waste listening to her respectable lies and abuse. It was information he needed.

She was none too pleased to be silenced and tightened her lips which trembled very slightly, though this was evidently a sign of age rather than emotion for she was very cool and sure of herself.

The Captain took the Vogel file from his drawer and extracted Mario Querci's statement, addressing himself to the lawyer.

'Perhaps you would ask the Signora to be so good as to answer a few questions which might help us with our inquiries.'

Heer translated. He showed no embarrassment or special interest in what he had to translate, apparently having no objection to anything he had to do or say provided it was paid for. The woman stared at the window until the first question should be referred to her in German.

'Did you know your daughter-in-law's parents?'

'Certainly not.'

'They weren't at the wedding?'

'The mother had died some months before.'

'And her father?'

'The father had made himself scarce long before that, leaving them penniless.'

'And isn't that why Hilde Vogel was obliged to stop studying and find work?'

'It may have been.'

'Hadn't they, in fact, been quite well-to-do up till then?'

'Quite possibly. The father was an architect. All I know is that that girl didn't bring a penny with her when she married my son. She knew what she was about, all right. I saw through her from the start and said so.'

'I imagine that until her mother died the daughter attempted to keep her in the style to which she was accustomed.'

'They tried to keep up appearances, if that's what you mean. In my opinion people should live within their income and content themselves with the lifestyle they can afford.'

'Even so, it seems to me odd that the daughter should have taken a job as a shopgirl if she had been well educated, whether she was obliged to interrupt her studies or not.'

'If you want to split hairs I suppose you could say that she managed Becker's business since he travelled a lot, but if you ask me she only got a position like that because there was something going on between those two.'

'Do you know where the father went when he left?'

'He came here, of course, as I'm sure you know since she followed him in the end.'

'Followed him in what sense?'

'She came out here to live with him since my home wasn't good enough for her, or rather, my standards were too high for her.'

'She told you she was coming to live with her father?'

'Certainly. And I can't say I was surprised. In my opinion they were two of a kind. I understand he dabbled in painting and no doubt thought of himself as another Gauguin, running off like that. Needless to say nothing came of it.'

'Does it seem likely to you that her father would have wanted her living with him if, as you say, he had abandoned his family and left them penniless for all those years?'

'It must be so, given that that's what happened.'

'It isn't what happened, Signora. Hilde Vogel never lived with her father but in a hotel, alone.'

'I'm afraid you must be mistaken. She hadn't the money.'

'It seems she had plenty of money.'

'Then she was up to no good.'

And the Captain, though he found himself automatically defending Hilde Vogel against this vicious woman, was obliged to remember that he had said the same himself.

'Is your son still alive, Signora?'

'No, he isn't. He died very young, of a brain hæmorrhage.'

'What was his occupation?'

'He lectured in law at the University of Mainz.'

'Leaving you and your daughter-in-law together in the house?'

'Yes.'

'What were her financial circumstances at that point? Your son provided for her?'

'The estate is entailed on the male heir as it always has been. She had a small income, as I have, until such time as she might marry again, and she had the right to live in the house for her lifetime.'

'Would such income as she had have permitted her to live elsewhere?'

'In my opinion, no. The upkeep of the house was paid for from the estate. The income was for her personal expenses only.'

Sooner or later they must come to the question of the male heir. By this time the Captain was convinced that Guarnaccia had been right and that this interview could only be concluded at the Medico-Legal Institute. He decided it was best to get all the other information he needed before dealing with that problem. Nevertheless, he noted before going on that the woman was volunteering no information about there being a child and he was going to want to know why.

'Tell me about this man . . . Becker, you said his name was, with whom you think your daughter-in-law was involved.'

'I don't think so, I know so. I have a pair of eyes in my head. What's more, he was a bad lot, in my opinion. The whole town knew that he was having an affair with his secretary who used to travel around with him on the pretext of work.'

'Was this before or after his supposed affair with your daughter-in-law?'

'Before or after?' The woman almost spat with disgust. 'He was playing around with both of them. It may have been just my daughter-in-law when she first went to work for him, but he soon took up with the other one again when she and my son married. As for afterwards—'

'Just a moment. Are you saying this affair went on when your son and daughter-in-law were newly married?'

'I'm not saying anything of the sort! Do you imagine I would have allowed a scandal like that in the family? I watched her every minute, I can assure you. And I did everything in my power to get my son to break with Becker. Marriage and family are more important than friendship.'

'Did you quarrel over it.'

'I simply tried to make him see reason.'

'So she was Becker's mistress before she met your son? There needn't be anything extraordinary in that. She presumably broke with Becker and decided to marry your son.'

'She knew which side her bread was buttered. Becker would never have married her.'

The Captain paused to leaf through Mario Querci's statement. When he found the page he wanted he looked up and asked: 'Becker's secretary, was she older than your daughter-in-law?'

'Some years older. No doubt that's why he—'

'Her name?'

'Ursula Janz.'

'Is she still living in Mainz?'

'No.'

'Where is she living?'

'I can't imagine why you expect me to know that. I've no idea.'

'When did she leave the town?'

'When Becker sold his business and left.'

'How long ago was that?'

'At least fourteen years.'

'Did they go off together?'

'I wouldn't know. He left first but that doesn't mean anything.'

'And your daughter-in-law?'

'She had already left, almost a year earlier.'

'Because you quarrelled about her receiving Becker?'

'I don't stoop to quarrelling with that sort of person. I merely made my feelings known. I'm sure you understand that under my own roof, in my son's home . . .'

'Who ran the household after your son's death?'

'I did, naturally, before and after. My son was accustomed to an orderly household.'

The Captain remembered the face in the passport photograph. Had she managed to regard her mother-in-law with that detached irony? He strongly suspected not. She had been so much younger then and left a widow under this grim woman's rule without sufficient means to escape, or even anywhere to go. She may have invented the story of joining her father out of pride. Or was it to cover up the fact that she expected Becker to join her? In any case he hadn't. So what had she lived on? Where did the money from Geneva come from? And where was Becker now?

'Since you say this man Becker was a friend of your son's, do you happen to have a photograph of him?'

'No.'

'Your son and he were never photographed together? What about the wedding, wasn't he there?'

'He was, despite my wishes.'

'Then he must have appeared on one or two of the photographs, surely?'

'He did. But after my son's death I had no desire to keep anything that would remind me of his unfortunate marriage.'

'You destroyed the photographs?'

'I did.'

Had Hilde Vogel done the same? They had found no trace of her former life among her belongings.

'How old would Becker be now?'

'I suppose in his mid-fifties.'

'Leaving aside his relationships with women, what sort of man is he?'

'Arrogant. If I tell you that his favourite phrase was "ninety-nine point nine per cent of people are fools . . ." He liked to manipulate people.'

'Including your son?'

'My son was a very intelligent man but a rigidly honest one. Becker used to say he was his only worthy chess opponent, they had played chess together ever since their University days. But in my opinion Becker just liked having him around as an audience.'

'An audience for what?'

'You might say for his practical jokes, except that there was nothing amusing about them. He liked to make fools of people and then point out to them how gullible they had been.'

'Did he ever do anything illegal?'

'Not strictly speaking but my son often warned him that he was playing with fire.'

'Did he heed the warning?'

'I doubt it. He was utterly contemptuous of other people.'

'Was he ever seen again in Mainz after he left?'

'Never, I'm glad to say.'

'I see. Would you excuse me for a moment?'

When he went into the anteroom next door he found the

Marshal blocking the doorway with his broad back. Sweeton was slumped in a chair with his hands thrust deep in his pockets, his face pale and sullen. The two men stepped outside and closed the door on him.

'I think,' the Captain said, 'that we now know who Hilde Vogel's grey-haired visitor was.' And he explained briefly about Becker. 'It ties in with Querci's account of her having a lover with another woman in his life.'

'You're not thinking of a crime of passion?' The Marshal looked dubious.

'Anything but. I'm thinking she may have been black-mailing him, though without knowing what he was up to I'm going to have trouble proving it . . .'

The Marshal still looked dubious.

'What do you want me to do with the boy?'

'Let him telephone his father and then get him something to eat. After that we're going to the Medico-Legal Institute.'

'You want me to come, too?'

'Yes . . . unless . . . You could try talking to Querci again.'

'He's still down in the cells?'

'Yes, and now we've got something on the grey-haired visitor he might talk.'

'I don't think so,' murmured the Marshal, 'Not yet. I think I'd better come with you, as you said. I could talk to Querci later if you think I should. We'd perhaps better clear up a few things first . . .'

The Marshal knew well enough that he would have to be the one to deal with Querci but he wasn't looking forward to it and he wasn't sure yet how to tackle it.

'I'll see to the boy,' he said, opening the door of the anteroom again. 'Are you hoping he'll identify his friend's body?'

'If that's who the dead boy is, yes. Either he or the grandmother. I'm going to have to broach the matter with her now and it's not going to be pleasant for her, though I must say she's a tough character.'

The woman was sitting exactly as he had left her and the lawyer was speaking to her quietly in German.

The Captain apologized again for his absence and sat down.

'Signora, I'm going to have to ask you to officially identify your daughter-in-law's body. If, when the magistrate gives permission, you want to remove her to Germany . . .'

'I see no need for that.'

'In that case, Avvocato Heer, perhaps you and I could discuss the arrangements for her burial here at some later date.'

'Certainly.'

'Thank you. Now, Signora, I'd like to know whether your son and daughter-in-law had a child.'

'They did.'

'A boy?'

'Yes.'

'And his name?'

'Christian. He was named after my son.'

'How old was he when his father died?'

'He had just turned two.'

'And his mother left shortly afterwards?'

'About two years later.'

'She didn't attempt to take the child with her?'

'She did, but naturally it was out of the question. She had no means of supporting him.'

'But surely the boy inherited from his father?'

'He will inherit at age twenty-five. In the meantime I am the trustee along with our family lawyer.'

'Why wasn't his own mother made trustee?'

'In the first place because she understood nothing of such matters and would have been incapable of taking necessary decisions regarding investments. In the second place because it was Vogel family money. It would hardly have been suitable to have it administered by an outsider.'

'You married into the Vogel family yourself, did you not?'

'Bringing with me a very considerable dowry. A large part

of the property which my grandson will inherit originally belonged to my father.'

'If your daughter-in-law had persisted in her attempt to take the child away, could you have stopped her?'

'I rather think so. I would have had him made a ward of court on the grounds of his mother's immorality and the fact that she could offer him no alternative home or means of support.'

'Did you threaten to do that—openly, I mean?'

'I am not in the habit of threatening people. I made my intentions known, if that's what you mean.'

'And she gave up?'

'She abandoned the child rather than remaining where she was to bring him up in a respectable home.'

'Were they very close?'

'In what way?'

'In the way that a child and his mother are normally close. Did she care for him herself up to the time she left?'

'To a limited extent. Naturally the child had a nurse.'

'Chosen by you?'

'The woman was already in my employ in another capacity and had proved an excellent nurse when my son was small.'

'After your daughter-in-law left did she have any further contact with the child?'

'None whatever.'

'Yet I understand she sent money to an account in a bank in Mainz each month. Was the money sent to you?'

'It was.'

'Was it a contribution to the child's upkeep?'

'Supposedly, though he had no need of it. Naturally, I never touched it. I transferred it to a savings account in my grandson's name.'

'Does he know about it?'

'I informed him of it on his eighteenth birthday.'

'Why was the money sent directly to the bank rather than to you personally?'

'At my request. I had no desire for any personal contact with my daughter-in-law.'

'You regard a cheque as a personal contact? Or were there letters, too?'

'In the first few years, yes.'

'You didn't answer them, apart from requesting her to send the cheque directly to your account?'

'The letters were not addressed to me but to my grandson.'

'Did he answer them when he was old enough?'

'He never saw them.'

'You considered you had the right to censor your grandson's mail?'

'My grandson was a small child. I considered myself responsible for his moral welfare since he had been left in my care.'

'And you felt his moral welfare would be endangered by receiving letters from his mother?'

'I did. And the manner of her death, not to mention the unexplained money which enabled her to live in a hotel, indicates that my fears were more than justified.'

The Captain watched Avvocato Heer carefully as he translated this last remark into Italian but the heavy face of the Swiss showed nothing but bland professional politeness. He decided against making any mention of his suspicions about blackmail but to stick to the subject of the boy.

'Does your grandson still live with you, Signora?'

'He does, though most of the time he is away at school in Frankfurt.'

'Is that where he is now?'

She hesitated for only a fraction of a second before saying, 'At the moment he's travelling.'

'In Europe?'

'I believe so. He sends me only the occasional postcard.'

'When did he leave Germany?'

'At the beginning of July.'

'Shouldn't he be back at school by now?'

'He should. Unfortunately he has inherited some of his mother's headstrong ways.'

'Do you think he may have come here to see his mother?'

'I have no reason to think so.'

'Not even the fact that your daughter-in-law ceased to send the regular cheques after July?'

'My bank manager deals with that. I was unaware of it.'

She was lying and not very successfully. There had to be a reason why she hadn't mentioned the boy until he had insisted.

'Has he ever been in trouble?'

'If you mean with the police, certainly not.'

'At school, then.'

She didn't answer immediately and there was a short discussion in German between her and the lawyer. Without understanding a word of it, the Captain was convinced that the lawyer had advised her to tell the truth on the grounds that it wouldn't be difficult to find out anyway.

'There was a problem at the college,' she said finally.

'Drugs?'

'Yes.'

'Did he run away?'

'I've already told you he is travelling.'

'Did he run away before the term ended? I can find out for myself,' he added to save the lawyer trouble, 'if you prefer it.'

'He left shortly before the end of term, yes. He had important examinations. Unfortunately, he's always been highly strung.'

'Apart from the problem of exams, was he unhappy?'

'My grandson has always had every comfort and every consideration. And if I may be allowed to mention it, I'm here to see that my daughter-in-law's affairs are properly settled and the family's interests protected, not to discuss my grandson.'

Which presumably meant that now Hilde Vogel was

dead and had left some money behind her she had at last become part of the family.

'Is there a will?' the Captain asked Heer.

'Yes. She left everything to her son apart from a small legacy to a man named Querci. I'm afraid I can't tell you anything about him but I imagine we'll be able to trace him.'

'We know who he is,' was the Captain's only comment on that.

'And if the boy leaves no heir, or if, for example, he didn't outlive his mother, was any provision made for that?'

'I advised my client to make such a provision. Should the son have failed to outlive his mother, this man Querci was to inherit. The estate was not entailed and once the son inherited, any further decisions rested with him.'

'Wouldn't a will like that be contested in the case of Querci's inheriting?'

'It could be, by any close blood relative, but I understand that my client had none.'

'Have you explained the situation to the Signora here?'

'I have.'

'If the boy inherited and died without making a will, would she inherit from him?'

'Quite probably. As far as I know, there would be no other claimants.'

'Have you also discussed that with her?'

'We have discussed all possible contingencies, though that particular one was touched on only briefly.'

'I see. Avvocato Heer, I have reason to believe that Christian Vogel died here in Florence before his mother, possibly from an overdose of drugs, though I have no proof of that. Unfortunately, the state in which the body was found will make his identification extremely difficult and also distressing. I'd be grateful if you would accompany the Signora when we take her to the Medico-Legal Institute.'

'By all means.'

'Thank you. Might I ask if you knew your client's father, the owner of the villa near Greve?'

'Yes, I did. I acted for him when he bought the house. In fact, it was only through her inheriting the property that I came to have his daughter as a client.'

'He left a will?'

'No, he didn't. It was only on my insisting that he gave me her address as his next of kin. He was very careless about his affairs and, as far as I know, had no interest in his daughter.'

'What did he live on?'

'On the income from some shares which his daughter also inherited. It was very little and certainly not enough for the upkeep of a place the size of his. I imagine the place must have been neglected.'

'You never saw it?'

'No.'

'How often did you see him?'

'Very rarely.'

'Did he take himself seriously as a painter, as far as you can judge?'

'I couldn't say. I got the impression it was a certain way of life he was interested in. He never spoke about his painting much and I doubt if he ever made anything from it.'

'When was the last time you saw him?'

'He sent for me when he was taken into hospital. He was in a very bad condition and I understand his liver was irreparably damaged.'

'He drank?'

'Very heavily. I had last seen him some years previously when the ten year limit was up on the payment of conveyance taxes on the villa. He was already in bad shape then.'

'And when he died you contacted his daughter?'

'Yes. She was surprised at first to have inherited the villa, until I explained that there had simply been no will and she was his only relative. Apparently she had made considerable efforts to make peace with her father when she arrived here but had been firmly rebuffed.'

But she'd never admitted it, the Captain mused, not to her mother-in-law to whom she had always given her father's address. Not even to Querci, to whom she had pretended he was dead.

'I wonder, in that case, how she knew where to find him, given that he had no further contact with his family after walking out on them.'

'She knew he was in Florence, or was fairly sure of it. The family had taken holidays here and he had always expressed a desire to live here. I gather she asked for help at the German Consulate and they got in touch with the Foreign Residents' Department at the Questura.'

Had Christian had to go through the same procedure to find his mother? The Captain strongly suspected not.

'Would you ask the Signora if her grandson, when informed about the money sent by his mother, asked for her address?'

It was obvious that the question displeased her.

'He did.'

'Did you give it to him?'

'I did not.'

'But he could have got it from the bank?'

'He could have done, yes.'

'Did you quarrel about it?'

'I've already pointed out that these questions regarding my grandson seem to me to be irrelevant.'

'Unfortunately, Signora, I have reason to believe that your grandson did come here to find his mother. We have evidence that a boy named Christian was staying in her villa. The boy disappeared during the summer and a body was subsequently found which could well be his. If I have troubled you with so many questions it was only in an attempt to verify that possibility. Had you been able to tell me that your grandson was at home, alive and well, I would have been able to spare you the distressing business of trying to identify the body and clothing of the boy we found dead. I'm very sorry, Signora, but that's now going to be necessary.'

Again that slight trembling of the lips.

'I'm sure you're mistaken.'

'I sincerely hope so.'

'You must be mistaken. My grandson . . . he would have had documents with him, his passport . . .'

'No documents were found. It's possible that death was caused by an accidental overdose of heroin and that his papers would have been removed by his companions to avoid any involvement. I have already asked Avvocato Heer to accompany you when we go to the Medico-Legal Institute. Perhaps you should try to eat something first.'

'No. This misunderstanding must be cleared up immediately . . . immediately. Wait . . . you said he disappeared in the summer?'

'Yes. We only found the body recently.'

'But that would mean—' Her face had reddened and her fists tightened around the black handbag on her knees.

'I'm afraid it does mean that identifying him, even for you—'

But she was interrupting, talking rapidly to the lawyer without giving him time to translate. When at last he managed to stop her he said:

'She wants to know, if it is her grandson, whether he must have died before his mother.'

Only then did the Captain begin to understand her reticence about the boy.

'A month before.' He saw and understood her relief as she heard the translation.

'Had he become violent?'

'He had begun to demand money, a great deal of money.'

'Did he threaten you in any way?'

'He . . . stole from me. Despite all my efforts he . . . even my Chinese vases, they were my mother's and he knew, he knew how I valued them and he stole them because I'd

refused him money. I was trying to help him and he stole
the very things that . . . They weren't the most valuable
things in the house. He did it to spite me and I was trying
to help him. There was no one I could turn to, you see. No
man in the house, no one whose advice I could ask, and I'm
an old woman, too old to know how to cope with a thing
like that.'

'You couldn't be expected to cope, Signora. He needed
professional help.'

'Professional help? Mainz is a small provincial city, Captain. If anyone had found out . . . I wanted to protect him.
I'd always tried to protect him.'

'Did all this begin when he was eighteen? When you told
him about his mother and the money?'

'I . . . perhaps. I hadn't thought of it but it must have
begun about then. Though he had always been difficult,
secretive. I was wrong, then, to tell him. I've always tried
to be fair, to do the honest thing, but in this world the
dishonest people always come off best. If you knew what
I've suffered in this past year! It was almost a relief when
he went. I didn't know him any more, he'd become a
stranger, almost a monster.'

'Were you afraid of him?'

She didn't answer at once. She was shaking her head as
though wanting to deny it and her thin hands were fumbling
at the clasp of her handbag. 'I beg your pardon.' She had
got the bag open but seemed to have forgotten what she was
looking for. Two big tears were rolling down her wrinkled
cheeks, making pink runnels in the white powder.

The Captain passed her a folded white handkerchief and
she accepted it, dabbing at her eyes and blowing her nose.

'I just wanted him to be successful and happy, to have
a clean respectable life like his father. You do understand?'

'I understand. Signora, it would be very helpful if you
would identify your daughter-in-law, but if it would be too
distressing for you to look at the body of the boy we found

we can establish whether or not it is your grandson through his dental records. It's what we would have done in any case had you not come to see me.'

'But that would take time . . .' She was twisting the damp handkerchief between her fingers, forgetting to wipe the tears that continued to flow.

'It would take time, yes.'

'Then I'd rather know now, while I'm here. If you'll just give me a moment to pull myself together . . .'

'Of course. Would you like to eat something before we go?'

'I couldn't, no. I'd like a glass of water.'

'I can have some brandy sent up if you'd prefer it.'

She shook her head.

The Captain rang for the water and then went next door. The Marshal was sitting, still and impassive. The boy, now bolt upright in his chair, looked frightened and agitated. Perhaps the telephone call to his home had made him more aware of the reality of his situation. When he saw the Captain he jumped to his feet.

'You can't keep me here, you'll see. My father's arriving tomorrow!'

The Captain ignored him, asking Guarnaccia, who stood up slowly, 'Has he eaten something?'

'Coffee and a sandwich.'

'Then let's go.'

They drove out to the Medico-Legal Institute in two cars, the Marshal travelling in the second one with Sweeton. When they left the mild warmth of the broad sunlit piazza and began to climb the steps in the cold shadow of the big building the boy suddenly stopped.

'You can't force me to go in there if I don't want to.' He said it, unthinkingly, in English. The Marshal, though he had understood anyway, said nothing. He simply blocked the boy's retreat with his much greater bulk and they moved forward again.

The chilly, marble-floored entrance hall smelled depressingly of formaldehyde.

'Keep him here for the moment.' The Captain indicated a shiny wooden bench. 'We'll deal with the identification of the woman first.' He went to speak to someone at the reception window and after a brief wait a porter led him off down a long corridor, followed by the old lady and the lawyer.

'Sit down,' the Marshal said to Sweeton, but he himself remained standing, his big eyes on the boy who looked as sick as if he had already seen a corpse.

The others weren't gone very long before the porter returned.

'This way.'

When they joined the group in the storage room it was discovered that there had been a mistake. The boy's body had been removed to the dissecting room on another floor. They were taken up by a different porter who told them, 'The Professor's starting work on it when he gets back from lunch.' They stepped out of the lift on a corridor where the smell was much stronger.

'In here.'

'Just a moment.' The Captain drew the man aside to speak to him. 'We think it may be this woman's grandson. If the body could be partly covered so that she doesn't see that the head . . .'

'That's all right. I brought him up myself. The cover's still on. Do you want the clothes sending up? It will save you some time.'

'Yes, if you can manage it.'

'I'll just check that there's somebody here to look after you.'

He opened the door of the dissecting room.

The waiting group had barely had time to glimpse one corner of the dissecting trench straddling a trough in the centre of a tiled floor when John Sweeton doubled over as if about to vomit. He didn't vomit. Instead he swung round, butting the Marshal in the stomach, and fled down the corridor, his head still low.

'I'll see to him.' The Marshal had foreseen his flight, if not the blow to his stomach, and had already checked where the staircase lay. The corridor was a dead end. He ran heavily after the boy, who skidded to a halt when he found no exit, turned to see the Marshal bearing down on him and crashed through a door on his left, slamming it behind him. There was a metallic clang followed by a splintering of glass on a tiled floor. When the Marshal reached the door he found it bolted on the inside.

The porter joined him.

'What's in there?' the Marshal asked him.

'It's just a store room. It takes some people in funny ways. He'll likely calm down if you leave him be for a bit.'

'He can't get out through there?'

'It's just a store room. There's no window in there even.'

'Leave me alone, I'll see to him.'

'If you're sure you can manage.'

'I'll see to him.' When he was alone the Marshal knocked softly on the locked door.

'No!' the voice was hysterical and almost unrecognizable. 'You can't make me go in there! You've no right!'

'And you've no right to shut yourself in there,' replied the Marshal stolidly.

'I'm staying in here as long as I want and you can't stop me!'

'I can break the door down.'

'You'll be sorry for this when my father gets here!' It was a child's voice saying childish things and the Marshal was pretty sure the boy was in tears.

'You father won't get here until tomorrow. Are you going to stay in there till tomorrow?'

'I don't care what you say, I don't want to see him and you can't force me!'

The porter reappeared by the Marshal's side. He was carrying some clothing wrapped in polythene bags.

'You don't seem to be calming him down.'

'I'm not trying to calm him down,' growled the Marshal. The porter left him.

'Listen to me,' said the Marshal loudly, his mouth close to the door. 'If you go on behaving like this you'll find yourself in worse trouble than you're in already.'

'I'm not in trouble! You can't prove anything and my father—'

'I said listen to me! Nobody knows yet how that boy died but if you go on like this we'll have every reason to think that you had something to do with it.'

'You're lying! You don't believe that, I had no reason to do it!'

'And how should we know whether you had a reason or not? You're giving us a reason to arrest you and after that, father or no father, it's going to take us a long time to prove what you did or didn't do—and you won't find prison any more comfortable than where you are now.'

When there was no answer the Marshal bumped his shoulder unhappily against the door which he had no intention of breaking down.

'Get away!' the boy shrieked.

'Open this door!'

'Wait ....' There was a scuffling noise, a crunching of glass, and the door opened slightly.

Instead of letting the boy out the Marshal pushed his way inside and shut the door again.

'What are you doing? Let me out of here!'

'A minute ago you wanted to stay inside.'

The room was dark except for a faint grey light coming from a ventilator connecting it with the one next door. The boy had backed into the far corner between wooden shelving full of glass bottles, some of which he had smashed when he blundered in there. The Marshal could feel a lot of broken glass underfoot and a gleaming metal bucket was overturned in the middle of the floor. The room stank of disinfectant. He took a step forward.

'Get away from me!' The boy was holding one of his hands as though it was hurt but it was impossible to see in the gloom whether or not it was bleeding. The Marshal picked up the overturned bucket and put it to one side.

'Don't come near me, I'm warning you—if you touch me . . .'

'That's enough . . .' The boy's pale face was just visible. His staccato breathing was that of a distressed child exhausted by crying. The Marshal was distressed himself. The only answer to this boy's problems was to get him home to his parents and off drugs. But he had already got himself in too deep for it to be that simple. It was too late, that was the trouble. It always was too late. If he had spoken his mind that night before they arrested Querci . . . But Querci had done what he did and nobody could change that. You couldn't do much to help people when it came down to it, and on top of that they looked at you as though you were the villain, like this boy was doing now. It would soon be Querci's turn to look at him in the same way. Well, he had wanted to frighten the lad and now he had.

The Marshal wasn't very good at the part he had decided to play and he stood there in the small dark room wondering what to do next. But the boy saw only the menacing bulk before him, its silence making it more menacing than ever.

'If I tell you what happened to Christian . . .'

The Marshal didn't trust himself to speak.

'You won't touch me . . .?'

'Tell me his name.'

'His name? I don't know, I swear to you, I only saw him that one time.'

'Christian's name, his surname.'

'I . . . I don't know . . . what does it matter? He never said.'

'It matters.'

'I don't know. We never bother about things like that. People just drift in and out. In any case, all of it was his idea.'

The boy sniffed and lifted both hands to his face to wipe it.

Seeing the dark smudge he left behind, the Marshal moved forward a little to get a closer look at the hand.

'Don't touch me! You promised . . .'

'What did I promise?' He stood still again.

'I'll tell you, I said I'd tell you . . .'

'Well?'

'It was Christian's idea, I swear it.'

'You've already said that. What idea?'

'About the woman who owned the villa. He said he could get money out of her.'

'To buy drugs?'

'Yes. He knew her. She was German like him.'

'And why should she give him money?'

'He knew something about her . . .'

'You mean he was blackmailing her?'

'It didn't start like that . . . We didn't—he didn't plan it. The first couple of times she just gave him money. I wasn't there, I swear it, I didn't know her. I never even saw her.'

'And she just gave him money.'

'She took him out for a meal as well. Maybe she . . . Anyway, it's true that she gave him money, he showed me the cheques. He said there was plenty more where that came from. Then the agent came up to the villa with an architect. They were going to do the place up.'

'Were you asked to leave?'

'No. At least, not until my contract ran out.'

'But Christian didn't have a contract, did he?'

'No. But he wasn't worried. He said she was doing the place up for him, that she expected to come and live there with him. I don't know if it was true or not. He was always making things up to make himself sound important. He was pretty crazy.'

'But you made friends with him. Do you speak German?'

'No. He could speak English, and French as well. He was brilliant at languages. Even so, he was crazy.'

'But you made friends with him,' insisted the Marshal.

'He was there, that's all.'

'And he gave you money.'

'He liked to make out he was somebody.'

'When your father arrives the Captain will want to know how much money he was sending you.'

After a pause the boy said, 'He'd stopped sending it.'

'He was angry with you?'

'I should have gone back in the spring to apply for University.'

'Didn't you want to go?'

'He wanted me to study law. I wanted to paint.'

'So you took money off Christian.'

'He lent me a bit, that's all.'

'Did he intend to live in the villa with the owner?'

'No. He said she was out of her mind if she thought he was going to bury himself in a dump like that with her. He said he was going to Amsterdam, that it was the best place to get dope, and he was going to get money off her to go, that she wouldn't dare refuse him because now he knew all about her and where her money came from.'

'How did he know?'

'He claimed she told him, but you could never tell when he was telling the truth and when he was fantasizing. Anyway, he said he'd arranged to meet her up near the fort and he asked me to take him because I've got a scooter. There are no buses back to Greve at night.'

'He promised you a cut?'

'He was going to lend me something, that's all. I didn't even know that woman!'

'All right. Go on.'

'When we got there I hid myself and the scooter.'

'Did the woman come alone?'

'She didn't come. A car drew up where Christian was waiting. The driver wound his window down to talk to him. It was a man.'

'Could you hear what they were saying?'

'I was too far away . . .'

The boy was cradling his wounded hand close to his chest. It must have been hurting him badly but the Marshal didn't dare make a move.

'Did Christian get into the car?'

'No. The man got out and they walked down the hill a little way. I followed them part of the way and hid again.'

'You still couldn't hear what was going on?'

'I was too far away. I didn't dare go any nearer. He'd never said anything about a man. He said the woman lived on her own. I thought it might have been a policeman. But then I saw him give Christian an envelope and then he . . . When Christian turned away the man got hold of him, he just got hold of him by the neck. There was no noise . . .'

'You didn't try and help him?'

'There was no noise. Just the crickets, and it was hot, I was sweating, soaked to the skin. There was no noise at all and there were houses all down one side of the lane with their shutters closed in the dark. It was as if nothing was happening. If Christian had called out . . . I saw his hands fly up and then they were still, both of them, for what seemed a long time. I didn't dare move . . .'

'You could have helped him.'

'I couldn't! I couldn't help him! If the man had seen me he'd have got me too! There were houses there, he should have screamed but there was no noise! He was crazy, I've told you, he was crazy, he should have screamed to make somebody come, screamed and screamed, and I couldn't . . . and the man bent over him . . . then he walked back up to his car and just drove away. I saw Christian in the ditch with his eyes open, staring at me . . .'

'Did you take his documents?'

'I didn't touch him, I ran up the hill and got my scooter. I could hardly stay on it because I was shaking so much. It was his fault, don't you understand? He should have screamed . . .!' He flung himself against the side of the wooden shelves with his head crooked in his arm, heaving long dry sobs. The Marshal backed slowly towards the door and opened it. He saw the grey tiles and the broken glass swimming in blood-streaked disinfectant, and heard the Captain's footsteps hurrying towards them along the corridor.

CHAPTER 10

'What's happened to him?'

'He cut his hand. We'd better get him over to the hospital and have it stitched. I'll call the porter to explain this mess . . . Have you finished?'

'Yes. I've sent them back in my car. The woman's in a bad way but she has identified the boy pretty conclusively, mostly by his hands and the leather bracelet. He'd worn it for years. We can manage without Sweeton seeing him.'

'I don't want to, don't make me . . .' From inside the store room Sweeton's voice had lost all its rebelliousness.

'Come on, let's get you out of here.' The boy allowed the Marshal to lead him out of the room without protest.

They left in the remaining car with its light and sirens going and drew up outside the nearby emergency hospital within minutes. The doctor who received them looked from the injured boy to their uniforms and asked, 'A road accident?'

'No.' The Captain offered no explanations. It would have taken too long. The doctor took the boy away without comment but looking none too happy about it. When he returned to where they were waiting he looked frankly suspicious. There was no knowing what the boy might have told him.

'He seems to be in shock. More so than those injuries could account for. What are you intending to do with him?'

It was a problem the Captain had been rapidly thinking over as they waited, having heard the Marshal's account.

He could arrest Sweeton on a charge of blackmail but he'd have trouble making it stick. The boy's father was an English judge and would go straight over his head to the Substitute as soon as he arrived, and he knew well enough how things would go from then on. But the boy was a key witness and a frightened one. If they let him go now and he vanished, the Substitute would be equally furious. And things were already going to be bad enough with those injuries to explain.

'It might be as well if you kept him here,' he said at last, 'at least until tomorrow.'

'This is an emergency hospital. We don't have beds to spare.'

'You said he was in shock.'

'He's not in danger. Where are his parents?'

'His father's arriving from England tomorrow.'

'Is this boy in trouble with you?'

'Yes, he is. And if you can't keep him it will probably have to be the prison hospital.'

'I see. In that case I'll keep him here under sedation until tomorrow. After that the father can take responsibility. In the meantime I need a written account of the cause of the injuries. You'll find the appropriate form at the reception desk.' He looked as though he would have liked to say more but two ambulances had drawn up outside and a nurse called to him as the first stretcher was wheeled in. With a curt nod he left them.

It was the Marshal who filled in the form. When he had finished he said, 'Now it's a question of whether the boy tells the truth when his father arrives.'

'Do you think he will?'

'I don't know.' The Marshal was fishing for his dark glasses as they approached the glass doors of the entrance. 'I don't know.'

Running away? What do you mean, running away?' the Substitute Prosecutor snapped. He had never made any secret of his preference for working with the police rather than the carabinieri and no doubt he now considered his opinions vindicated. The Captain held the receiver a little further from his ear as the tirade continued unabated.

'And who is this Marshal who was supposed to have him in charge?'

'Guarnaccia, sir, Stazione Pitti.'

'Guarnaccia? Guarnaccia? I've heard that name, has he been in trouble before?'

'Certainly not. He's often been exceptionally helpful.'

'Has he? Well, he's been exceptionally unhelpful this time. You realize that this boy's father is a judge and that when he gets here there's going to be trouble. Why wasn't he properly guarded?'

'He wasn't under arrest, sir, and the men I have are fully occupied on another case—'

'I'm not interested in other cases! I'm interested in this case and I want a full report of this whole business before the father gets here tomorrow. Where's the boy now?'

'Under sedation in the hospital.'

'Get a man out there immediately to stand guard! If he gets out and disappears before his father arrives—'

'I've already done that. Of course, if you'd care to sign the warrant we can arrest him on a charge of blackmail.'

'You'll do nothing of the sort! I'll deal with this—and you'd be better employed getting some concrete evidence against this man Querci. If you knew your job you'd have got him to talk before now.'

Especially, thought the Captain grimly, as he hasn't a father who's a judge and might take exception to a few bruises. He could have defended himself, as far as evidence was concerned, by telling the Substitute about Hilde Vogel's will, but he didn't. He was going to wait for Guarnaccia. However long it took, he was going to wait, Substitute or no Substitute, because if he'd had the sense to give the man a hearing in the first place . . .

On the way back from the hospital the Marshal had

mumbled apologetically, 'It was my fault, I should have spoken out before you arrested him. It would have made things that much easier. If I'd known he needed money . . . but he seemed content enough to me.'

'He was. It was his wife who'd wanted to get him out of hotel work after that business in Milan. She wanted him to buy into her father's shop.'

'I see. I didn't know. Only it seemed obvious that if he didn't take anything from the room . . . Well, I should have spoken out.'

'And I should have thought of it myself.'

He hadn't minded admitting that, but he could hardly admit that he'd been glad enough to let Guarnaccia go that night before the Substitute arrived. Getting out of the car at Pitti the Marshal had said, 'They have children, don't they?'

'One. A little girl.'

'I'll be with you as soon as I've finished. I'll take Lorenzini with me.'

Now, at last, the Substitute was coming to the end of his tirade, since the Captain, his mind elsewhere, was answering 'yes, sir' and 'no, sir', giving him no fuel for further attack. At the end of it he hung up, feeling rather better than otherwise. He'd done his best to avoid this sort of clash, as he did with all magistrates, but now that it had happened anyway he felt free to get on with the job in his own way and to let Guarnaccia get on with it in his. He pulled the Vogel file towards him and opened it. With luck he had about two hours before he would be interrupted, and now he had all the information he needed apart from what Querci would shortly give him. He opened the grey passport and met that cool, ironic glance once again. Not blackmail, it couldn't have been that. Whatever it was, everything had changed when her son arrived, a repetition of her own arrival all those years ago. But this time the roles were reversed. It was the son who didn't want to know. One thing, at any rate, was certain. Whatever Hilde Vogel had been up to all those years, if she'd carried on with it, been as stubborn and cold-hearted as her father, she would probably have still been alive today and so would her son. That moment of maternal affection, or sentimentalism, her attempt to make up for a miserable past, had resulted in worse disasters than most crimes ever did. The page from the newspaper where the unidentified body in the Arno was reported was also in the file. Maestrangelo read it. He read it again, frowning. Then a faint smile crossed his face as though he thought himself absurd for what he was thinking.

Nevertheless, still looking at the newspaper, he picked up the telephone receiver and asked for a call to be put through to a German colleague with whom he had worked for over six months on a kidnapping case the previous year. He wasn't the right person to ask but at least they managed to understand each other in a mixture of Italian and English and he would push the request on to the right quarter. It took some time for the man to be found, but when his booming voice finally answered it conjured up an instant picture of the big man with gingery hair whose fair-skinned face used to turn bright red after the first glass of wine. He was an exceptionally clever policeman whose bearlike appearance gave him the added advantage of looking harmless and a bit stupid. His first reaction to the Captain's request was surprise.

'There was nothing in the papers here about it.'

'There was precious little here. I know I shouldn't really be asking you . . .'

'Of course you should! I'm delighted! Let me write the name down . . . Becker, you said?'

'Walter Becker. I'm pretty sure there won't be anything at all on your records but it's better to check.'

'And you could use some background information, I expect?'

'I'd be very grateful for anything, if it's possible.'

'Where did he live?'

'Mainz.'

'Mainz. I'll get on to them right away. Same number, same office?'

'Yes.'

'You can't imagine how I miss Italy. I bet it's still warm there even now.'

'Fairly.'

'You don't know when you're well off! It's been raining and blowing for over a week here and half my men are down with some sort of 'flu. I'll ring you back.'

After hanging up the Captain began a systematic reading of all the statements in the Vogel file, making notes for his own report to the Substitute as he went along. The expected interruption came after only an hour when one of his plainclothes lads came in and placed a small packet on his desk.

'We've got him, sir.'

Thank goodness for that. If ever he had needed all his concentration on one case it was now.

'Take it to the lab yourself. I'd like the analysis before we bring him in, if possible. Have you found out where he lives?'

'No chance of that, sir, but I'm meeting him in the piazza at ten tonight. He's giving me some of this stuff to push.'

'Go to Lieutenant Mori. He'll get your warrant. He can go with you tonight and I want at least three other men there.'

He gave the rest of his instructions and tried to share in the lad's enthusiasm. After all, the boys on this case were young and had done a good job. What was the use of depressing them with a reminder that for every supplier or pusher they picked up, another would quickly take his place?

'You've done well,' he said eventually, 'But remember, you haven't finished until you've got him in here. Above all, be careful. That appointment could be an ambush for you too, despite all our precautions, and if it is it won't be that easy to get help to you in time. It only takes seconds to knife somebody or push him into a car.' And he wouldn't be the first to be beaten to death or stabbed on a job like this.

'I'll be careful, sir.'

'Go and get some rest when you've seen the Lieutenant and dropped this at the lab.'

And with that problem out of the way the Captain settled down to work again, only pausing occasionally to glance at Hilde Vogel's photograph or at the window, wondering how soon Guarnaccia would arrive.

'Take your shoes off,' the Marshal suggested, 'or we'll be in more trouble for making a mess.'

Lorenzini sat down on the edge of the bath to undo his laces.

'It seems an unlikely place.'

'It's the only place left. It's got to be here somewhere. Wait, I'll move this stuff.'

The Marshal took all the bottles and a glass with two toothbrushes from the shelf of the bathroom cabinet and put them in a corner on the floor. 'Up you go.'

Lorenzini balanced himself precariously on the edge of the bidet and peered behind the glass cabinet.

'I can't see anything.'

'We might have to take it down.'

'But it's screwed to the wall.'

'The hooks will be but you should be able to lift the cabinet off them.'

'Balanced like this it won't be easy . . . Just a minute, it might come forward a bit . . .'

The top of the cabinet slid forward about a centimetre and something dropped a little way behind it.

'It's coming . . . Push it back now and slide the lower edge forward . . . There it is. Hold still, I've got it. Right. You can get down.'

When they had tidied up they came out through the bedroom. It had taken on a different character now that it was occupied by other people. Two brightly coloured raincoats lay across the bed and there were maps and a guide to Rome on the dressing-table along with a box of some foreign breakfast cereal. The manager of the Riverside was waiting out in the corridor, ill-tempered and anxious at the thought that his guests might turn up before they had finished.

'It's all right,' the Marshal said, 'we've finished. You won't be seeing us again.'

'I take it you found what you were looking for?'

But the Marshal volunteered no information.

About half an hour later he was sitting alone in the Querci's kitchen, balanced on a formica chair that was too small for him. He was staring out of the window at an identical window in the block across the street. The afternoon had turned grey and overcast and the atmosphere of the tiny room was dismal. The remains of a hasty cold lunch cluttered the draining-board. The Marshal's hat lay on the formica table next to the typewriter. The little girl, he knew without turning to look, was still peering at him through the crack in the slightly open door. The only voices came from the next flat.

Signora Querci came in with a packet in her hand.

'It was where you said, on top of the wardrobe.'

She didn't appear to have been crying but her face and her whole body had sagged and she looked older than her years. The Marshal got up and took the package. At the door the little girl spoke in a sudden, high-pitched voice. 'Where's my dad?'

'I've told you, he's in the hospital,' her mother said quickly, knowing that the question hadn't been for her.

But the child, unbelieving, kept her eyes fixed in accusation on the Marshal. He was so put out that he turned and walked down the interminable flights of stairs, afraid that they would both stand staring at him while he waited for the lift.

The call came through from Germany at a quarter to six in the evening. The sky had darkened prematurely with heavy clouds and the Captain had switched on his desk lamp.

'Maestrangelo? I'm sorry it's taken so long but, as you thought, there was nothing in our records so I got on to Mainz right away. The trouble was finding somebody who remembered him. In the end somebody suggested a man who retired from the Force four years ago and of course it took time to get in touch with him. It seems your man was quite a character.'

'Was his business sound?'

'Oh, nothing wrong with his business. Import-export. He had offices in Frankfurt but his warehouses were in Mainz, which was his home town. He had a shop there, too.'

'What did he deal in?'

'A bit of everything except food and industrial supplies. Leather goods, jewellery, porcelain, that sort of thing. Oh, and at one time he bought inlaid marble from Carrara, finished pieces to be made into tables over here. All very profitable.'

'Any ideas as to why he gave it up?'

'None at all. But it certainly wasn't business problems. The firm's still going strong, though it's expanded now and deals with a lot of lower quality stuff which Becker never touched. He liked quality, and he was shrewd, too, by all accounts, very cool.'

'Anything on his personal life?'

'Plenty. Mainz is a smallish place and he was a wealthy and influential man, well-known if not well-liked. At one time he was apparently keeping two mistresses quite openly but he obviously wasn't one to lose his head in those matters either. He didn't marry either of them. There were rumours that he was what you might call "kinky".'

He said it in German. When the Captain didn't understand he groped for an English or Italian equivalent and then explained, 'Odd sexual tastes. I don't know any details and it might well be just rumour. It wasn't that, anyway, that made him unpopular but another of his strange habits.'

'His practical jokes?'

'You already know about them?' He sounded disappointed.

'I hardly know anything, only that he indulged in them.'

'Well, some of them had quite serious repercussions, especially at the time when he'd got himself on to the Town Council. He somehow got a story going round that a certain very influential member of the Council was suffering from a fatal disease and immediately all sorts of secret meetings and re-alignments began. Whenever the subject came up Becker himself was careful to say it was probably an unfounded rumour. The unfortunate victim had no idea why he was losing supporters while new alliances were springing up all around him. When the truth came out he was so disgusted by his colleagues' behaviour that he resigned, which according to Becker proved that rumour was more powerful than truth.'

'You mean he admitted it?'

'He always did. It was never enough for him to manipulate people, he liked an audience—and after all, he'd denied the truth of the story all along. There were dozens of similar tricks but most of them didn't cause serious damage like that one, they just left people feeling foolish.'

'Nobody ever prosecuted him?'

'Nobody wants to admit their gullibility in public. Besides, it seems people were rather frightened of him. No doubt the worthy citizens of Mainz were relieved when he left.'

'Your man had no ideas as to where he went?'

'Only rumours again—and who knows whether they were started by Becker himself! Anyway, Amsterdam and New York seemed to be the most popular speculations. So, do you think he's the one?'

'I'm sure of it. It would take his sort of arrogance and brains.'

'I don't suppose he'll ever set foot in Germany again so I won't get a go at it. You're lucky, you'll make quite an international stir if you catch him.'

'I would, but I doubt if I or anyone else will catch him. Thank you for your help, anyway. And if it's any consolation to you, it's about to start raining here, too.'

The German roared with laughter. 'That little river of yours has to fill up sometime! Drink a good bottle of Chianti for me—and let me know what happens. Good luck!'

It began raining almost immediately, lightly at first, then insistently in a steady rhythm. The tall window in the Captain's office became blurred with raindrops which rolled down in a zigzag pattern because of little gusts of wind. He got up and walked over to look out but it was hardly possible to see anything. He followed the path of a big raindrop that trickled sideways and joined itself to a smaller one. He had all the facts written down in chronological order but what mattered was to present the report in such a way as to convince the Substitute. It would probably take him days to write. This rain had settled in for the duration. It would strip bare all the trees on the big avenues surrounding the city and churn up the smooth green river to a swollen brown flood. The city itself would be enveloped in a heavy mist for weeks, with only the golden globe on top of the cathedral dome clearly visible. It would go on until the middle of November and when it stopped it would be winter. Maestrangelo shivered at the thought, though the office was warm.

He recognized the knock on the door when it came. 'Come in, Marshal.'

Guarnaccia was enveloped in an enormous black raincoat. There were drops of moisture on the shoulders and on the hat he held in front of him. He seemed slightly out of breath but, as usual, the expression on his face told nothing. The first thing he did after laying his hat on the desk and removing the raincoat was to unbutton the top pocket of his uniform and drop the contents in front of the Captain. Only then did he sit down, still breathing heavily.

'Where was it?' Maestrangelo asked.

'Behind the bathroom cabinet.'

'Hm . . .' The Captain ran a finger lightly over the necklace. 'And to think that, after all, it's worthless . . .' When the Marshal said nothing he went on: 'Did you ever think it odd, the fact that she was undressed but still wearing these?'

'I didn't think about it at all. I don't know anything about that sort of thing.'

'But you're a married man.'

The Marshal only looked embarrassed.

'Well, I'm no expert on women and their jewellery but I should have thought she'd have taken this stuff off before undressing in normal circumstances.'

'I suppose so.'

'Only the circumstances, it seems, were not so normal. Probably Querci will enlighten us. There was nothing else in the rooms?'

'No. But there's this.' From a larger pocket Guarnaccia drew out the packet that Signora Querci had given him. 'I went to Querci's house.'

'And removed this? Without a warrant?'

'I didn't need a warrant,' said Guarnaccia blandly. 'I just talked to his wife and she found it and gave it to me.'

Of course. And if Guarnaccia had been the one to talk to her the first time . . . Well, it was no use thinking on those lines now. He had allowed himself to be pressurized by that wretched Substitute and had no one to blame but himself.

'Did she look inside it?'

'I've no way of knowing but I don't think so. I don't think she wants to know. I think she's going to apply for a legal separation right away.'

The Captain looked surprised. 'She seemed very fond of him, in spite of everything.'

'She is. You could hardly call it her own decision. More like that of her parents and the hotel manager, who's some sort of cousin. It seems they came to see her all together with a lawyer. She's going to need help and they made it clear that they won't help her unless she leaves him.'

'She might change her mind once she's over the shock.'

'I don't see how she can. There's the child to consider.'

'I suppose you're right.' The Captain was feeling the packet as he opened it. 'Photographs, I imagine . . .'

When the pictures were spread on the desk it was the incongruity, more than anything else, that was disconcerting. The Captain was chiefly interested in those which showed Hilde Vogel with her little boy. One was obviously taken after the christening since the baby was in a long white dress which looked antique. There were wedding photographs, too, in white cardboard folders with crimped and silvered edges, but only of the couple themselves. The elder Signora Vogel was noticeably absent, as was the ironic smile that had become so habitual in Hilde Vogel's later years. As for the other photographs . . . they couldn't be called pornographic. Erotic, rather, and artistic, too. Maestrangelo was no great expert in photography but it was easy to see that the lighting and composition were strikingly original, and he would have been willing to bet that Becker had developed them himself. It was becoming increasingly obvious that whatever the man turned his hand to, he did it brilliantly. Little wonder he thought so little of his fellow men.

He spread the photographs out and regarded them for a moment. The background was always the same, more or less, rumpled silk or velvet in a single brilliant colour.

'The way you would photograph a piece of jewellery . . .'

Only in this case it was a human body decorated with glittering stones and sometimes taken from such a height as to make it seem indeed like some tiny jewelled and sculpted figurine set on rich fabric to show it off. Others were close-ups, a white curve against black velvet, diamond pinpoints of light against a deep curving shadow. The Marshal's slow, regular breathing was the only sound in the half-lit room. There was no point, Maestrangelo decided, looking up, in asking Guarnaccia what he thought of the pictures since he would certainly reply that he didn't know anything about that sort of thing. Instead, he asked him. 'Why should Querci take this stuff?'

The Marshal dug ponderously into yet another pocket. 'I thought it might get lost, so I took it out . . . it's so small . . . there.'

So small as to be pitiful. A head and shoulders photograph of Querci that had obviously been cut out of a group snapshot. Almost certainly, his wife and child, if not other relatives, too, had been on the photograph, and he had probably had trouble removing it from the family album without his wife's catching him at it.

'It couldn't have been an excuse, you see, his going back that day for his shoes. Nobody knew about the seals being taken off.' He looked at his watch. 'I don't think there's anything else. I ought to get back. It's time my Brigadier went off duty and I expect the Substitute will want my written report on the Sweeton boy.'

'If you could spare another half-hour or so, I'm going through the whole file. It's almost certain that the Substitute will have Querci brought up for questioning tomorrow.'

'So soon?'

'I'm sure of it, and if he goes all out for murder with robbery as the motive it'll mean life.'

They were both looking at the necklace.

'I'll call Lorenzini,' the Marshal said.

By the time they finished it was quite dark outside the Captain's window except for a misty pink glow hanging over the city and dots of yellow light glimmering through the rain. Maestrangelo stood there looking out while the Marshal buttoned up his raincoat and adjusted his hat.

The worthless piece of jewellery was still lying on the desk.

CHAPTER 11

It wasn't the Captain's fault that things went the way they did. Even so, he couldn't help feeling satisfied. The whole procedure, as far as he was concerned, had been perfectly correct. He had informed the Substitute first thing the next morning of such new developments as there had been, chiefly the business of Hilde Vogel's will and the finding of the necklace and the photographs, and for the first time, the Substitute had appeared grudgingly pleased with him. As for the rest, it was mostly supposition anyway and though it would all appear in his written report it had no direct bearing on Querci's case, which was the only thing that interested the magistrate at that point. Whatever had passed between him and the English judge who had arrived that morning, it was unlikely that the Captain would be told much about it. By the following autumn John Sweeton would almost certainly be studying law at some English university, following sedately in his father's footsteps. If he were ever to be called as a witness it wouldn't be at Querci's trial but at another which was never likely to take place.

The appointment had been fixed for three-thirty in the Substitute's office at the Procura. When Maestrangelo had insisted on the presence of Marshal Guarnaccia it hadn't gone down too well.

'I frankly don't see the need.'

'It was he who found the necklace, and the photographs, too.'

'We have his written report, have we not?'

'Yes. But we have no proof. If we'd caught Querci with the necklace on him it would be different. As it is, there's nothing to say it wasn't there all the time. There isn't even a usable print on it. We can hope that when Querci sees we've found it he'll confess, but if he doesn't we have only Guarnaccia's theory to go on, and in that case I'd prefer him to be present.'

And Maestrangelo had got his way.

As a consequence, the magistrate's office was quite crowded. Querci sat facing the Substitute Prosecutor across a wide antique desk, a carabiniere guard behind him on each side. The Substitute's registrar sat a little to one side, ready

to record the proceedings, and the young lawyer who had
been provided for Querci sat beside his client, fidgeting with
the papers which he held balanced on the briefcase on his
knees. Maestrangelo stood behind the Substitute's chair
with a huge oil painting in a heavy gilt frame on the wall at
his back. Guarnaccia, as was his habit, had backed himself
into a corner where, in the shadow of a ceiling-high bookcase, he could observe everything with his big, slightly
protruding eyes, and where everyone except Maestrangelo
could forget his presence.

They might have been there to recite some play, the only
difference being that, though they all had the same script,
they each had a totally different idea of what the outcome
would be.

Maestrangelo toyed with this idea while the official pre-
liminaries were being got through. At that point he had no
intention of interrupting the Substitute, who was conducting
the scene with the confidence and panache that had got him
so far in his career so quickly. He assumed it would be
Querci himself, once he saw the evidence that lay on the
desk in two labelled envelopes, who would make a complete
confession without further difficulties. If that wasn't how it
turned out it was surely the fault of the Substitute himself,
whose arrogant brilliance might make a good show in court
but reduced a wretch like Querci to terrified silence. He had
a habit, which Maestrangelo found infuriating, of waving
his hands about in elegant, dramatic gestures as though he
were wearing his gown with its wide sleeves. Today he was
wearing a three-piece grey suit, and Maestrangelo, looking
down on him from behind, kept catching glimpses of the
fine white shirt cuffs against his long brown hands as he
gesticulated.

Another annoying habit which the Captain had observed
on many previous occasions was that of suddenly throwing
himself back in his chair and with upraised arms crying,
'My dear so-and-so, you're surely not asking me to
believe—'

There he went now . . .

'My dear Querci, you're surely not asking me to believe you weren't this woman's lover?'

Querci didn't answer. How could he have answered when the question, if that was what it was supposed to be, was put in that way? In the short time he had spent in a cell he had lost weight, especially around his neck. His eyes had a dazed look as though he no longer cared to focus them.

The last person Maestrangelo remembered seeing in that chair had been an old lag with a sharp Florentine tongue in his head who had given as good as he got, and the Substitute had enjoyed himself hugely. Querci's refusal to play the game, to feed him lines on which he could improvise brilliantly, was beginning to annoy him. Occasionally, with exaggerated courtesy, he would permit the defence lawyer to speak, never interrupting or contradicting him but waiting in expectant, bright-eyed silence for a long time after the young man had finished speaking as if to say that there must surely be something more intelligent or pertinent to follow. When nothing did, a faint puzzled smile would cross the Substitute's face and he would resume his questioning with pained gravity, as though the interruption had been a waste of everyone's time. It was a technique which never failed even with experienced lawyers who had learned to expect it. This time the unfortunate young man had lost his grip on himself and the case within the first ten minutes.

The Captain was more aware of his own tiredness than of anything that was passing in the room which, in his opinion, was overheated. That might just be his tiredness too. He had gone on working the previous night long after Guarnaccia had left, typing four and a half pages dealing with Querci's case and then the embryo of a second report which he had discussed with no one except his German colleague and the Marshal. Not long after he had finished, they had brought in the newly arrested drug supplier and he had been over an hour dealing with that. Needless to say, Galli had been on the scene well before his fellow reporters, bursting at the seams with food and wine, opinions and advice, and they had ended by having a whisky together in the Captain's office at heaven knows what hour. No doubt the whisky had also contributed something to his present vague muzziness.

'On the night in question you were on duty alone?'

'Yes . . .'

'Would you mind speaking up.'

'Yes. Alone.'

'At what time did you go up to visit the deceased woman?'

'I didn't . . . I didn't see her. I didn't see anything.'

'We know that you were in the habit of visiting this woman's room. You have already admitted to a relationship with her that could hardly have developed in the foyer. I quote: "I used to massage her neck when she had a head-ache." Do you now deny that statement?'

'I didn't see her that night.'

The Substitute inclined his head slightly to the left. 'Avvocato, would you be kind enough to inform your client that he must answer the questions put to him.'

The young lawyer murmured something in Querci's ear but the latter gave no sign of having heard or understood him. Nevertheless, when the question was repeated he answered: 'No, I don't deny it.'

'And did you massage her neck in the foyer? Behind your counter, perhaps?'

'No.'

'Thank you. You also, according to a statement made by the day receptionist, made a pet of this woman's dog. The animal was not permitted to wander about the public rooms and especially not in the foyer since the hotel did not normally allow pets of any sort. You were on duty at night. Are you asking me to believe that she brought the dog down to visit you in the middle of the night? In the small hours of the morning?'

'No . . .'

'I must ask you again to please speak up. Did she bring the animal downstairs to pay you social calls during the night?'

'No.'

As if he hadn't heard the first time! There were hardly two feet between them. The Captain was more than ever repelled by these methods. So much so that he was surprised the Substitute couldn't sense the waves of disgust hitting the back of his neck. Not that he would have cared . . .

'Did you meet outside the hotel?'

'No! Never . . . never.'

'In that case, my dear Querci—' he threw himself back in the chair with a light laugh—'you visited her room!'

For the first time Querci looked hesitatingly at his lawyer whose existence he had barely acknowledged until then, but the Substitute gave him no time to speak.

'Yes or no, Querci, yes or no! Did you visit her room?'

'Yes.'

'Ah!'

And that was that. Instead of the expected question about the night of the murder, he suddenly changed tack, picked up one of the envelopes and, with a sweeping gesture emptied its contents on to the desk, swooped on the tiny photograph and flourished it under Querci's nose.

'You recognize it?'

'I . . . yes, of course.'

'Of course! It's a picture of you, isn't it?'

'Yes.'

'I wouldn't want to make a mistake on that point. You see, it's important! A picture of you, Querci—who took it?'

'My wife.'

'Your wife? She wasn't on the picture, then? There were other people on it, I imagine, before you cut it up?'

'My in-laws . . . and Serena.'

'Serena?'

'My little girl.' Querci's eyes were focused now and filling with tears. His face was deep red.

'Very touching. Of course it would be more convincing if it weren't for the fact that you cut your little girl off the picture so that you could give it to your mistress!'

'She wasn't . . . it wasn't like that . . .'

'Then tell us how it was, Querci.'

'I . . . nothing . . . She asked me for a photograph and I saw no reason . . . only I didn't have one, not just of me. There was no harm in it. She was a lonely person.'

'Exactly! And not only was she lonely, she was rich. What better opportunity was a night porter likely to come across!'

'It wasn't—'

'It wasn't like that, as you keep on saying. But we now know that that's exactly how it was, Querci, because we now know about the will!'

Querci's lawyer gave a visible start and then shot his client a resentful glance. But Querci himself was utterly confused.

'I don't understand you . . .'

'Then I'll explain. This woman left you money—and since, by a coincidence very fortunate for you, her son happened to be killed shortly before she herself was killed, you inherit everything.'

Querci looked from one to the other of the faces around him as if trying to understand what was happening. 'I didn't know. I didn't know . . .'

'What didn't you know? About the will? About the son?'

'The will. I didn't know! I swear it!'

'A moment ago you were swearing you'd never been to that woman's room, Querci, so how can you expect anyone to believe you now?'

Without giving him time to reply, the Substitute suddenly spread the photographs of the naked Hilde Vogel fanwise, like a conjuror. He didn't speak. Querci's eyes scanned them quickly but shifted almost immediately to the other, unopened, white package.

'Look at these photographs, please,' snapped the Substitute. 'Look at them carefully. Have you seen them before?'

'I . . . yes.'

'Did you take them?'

'No!'

'You're not looking at them. You're impatient to know what's in the other package? We'll come to that. I'm asking you about these photographs.'

'I didn't take them.'

'Who did?'

'He did . . . somebody she knew. It was years ago, in Germany.'

'What time did you go to see her that night?'

'I didn't.'

'Then let's satisfy your curiosity!' And he snatched up the other package and tipped the necklace on to the photographs.

'Do you recognize this as the property of Hilde Vogel?'

There was a silence so profound that the rain could be heard falling in the courtyard outside. The Substitute was leaning forward, his forearms flat on the desk, his back rigid. He didn't repeat the question. Nobody in the room moved. Querci continued to stare at the necklace in silence, and then in silence, very slowly, he began to shake his head.

'No,' he said at last. 'No.'

And that was when the Captain knew he had to intervene. He took a step forward and bent to murmur something in the Substitute's ear. The latter looked up sharply and then hesitated, but only for seconds. After all, when the case came into court he would be the only one there to take the credit. Swinging sideways in his chair, he inclined his head and waved the Captain on as though he were traffic. But the Captain stepped back to his place without a word. Judging by the faces of all the others in the room, it might have been the bookcase itself that had suddenly decided to speak when the Marshal stepped forward.

'It wasn't hers, was it?'

'No.' Querci met the Marshal's expressionless stare like someone hypnotized.

'It belonged to Walter Becker?'

'I never knew his name.'

'But you know who I mean?'

'Yes.'

'And who came back the night she was killed and went up to her room. You didn't want to tell us that because the necklace was his, wasn't it?'

'If it had been hers I wouldn't have—'

'Of course not. He used to dress her up in that sort of stuff and when she was younger he used to take photographs, photographs like these, is that right?'

'He was a bit weird. She told me about it.'

'During your little chats. I imagine she used to ring for you during the night and you would go up to her room?'

'It's true—but even so there was nothing—'

'It doesn't matter. She rang for you that night, or somebody did, and you went up in the service lift. When you got there, there was nobody there. Did you realize what had happened?'

'No! If I had . . .'

'She was dead by then. You know that by now. He took her down to his car in the other lift as soon as he'd got you away from your desk.'

'I didn't know! How could I have?'

'But you must have known she was afraid, of Becker and of her son.'

'Even so, I never thought . . . When they found her in the river I was sure she'd killed herself because of what had happened with the boy.'

'What happened?'

'That was when it all started, when he came. It's true that I didn't know she had a son. In all those years she'd never said. Then he turned up. She was so agitated and she had nobody to tell except me. That was when she showed me the photographs—not those, I'd already seen those, but the ones of her husband and the little boy. When he turned up she changed completely. She wanted to make a new life for herself and the boy. She talked of nothing else. She said it would make up for everything.'

'Did she tell you the truth about her father?'

'No. She didn't explain herself. She was very agitated and she talked more about the future than the past.'

'She intended to break off with Becker?'

'Yes, she wrote and told him so.'

'And he came to see her?'

'Yes. It was the first time he'd ever been, I wasn't lying. But by the time he arrived everything had changed.'

'Because she'd found out the boy was an addict?'

'Not just that. All he wanted from her was money. She said he hated her for having abandoned him. In the end she was afraid of him. He'd asked her for an enormous sum and said he'd leave if she gave it to him.'

'Did she believe him?'

'I don't think so. In any case she was terrified.'

'Did she admit to you that he was blackmailing her?'

'Blackmailing? No, just that he demanded money. It's not the same thing.'

'As demanding money with menaces? No. But that's what he was doing. She was frightened, you say, so I suppose when Becker arrived she told him?'

'She'd decided to give him the money in the hope that he'd really go.'

'But she was afraid of him and she let Becker go and meet him in her place?'

'Yes. He took cash. That was the end of it. She never heard from the boy again. After that Hilde resigned herself to going on with the old life.'

'Where was the necklace that night? On the bed?'

'On the floor.'

'You've never stolen anything in your life before, have you?'

'No.'

'What on earth did you intend to do with it?'

'I didn't think, not then. I just saw it lying there . . . Afterwards I thought of selling it at one of those auctions they do on the private TV stations, but I didn't even know how to go about it.'

'It's worthless, do you know that?'

Querci only stared at him, uncomprehending.

'It's worthless,' the Marshal repeated. 'Junk.'

There was silence for a moment. The registrar and Querci's lawyer were both writing rapid notes. It was Querci himself who broke the silence. Perhaps he wanted to get it over with.

'I knew you hadn't found the photographs, or you would have . . . That day when I came in for my shoes and heard about the seals being removed I went up there. I knew she kept them hidden but I wasn't sure where.'

'Nobody saw you go up?'

'Nobody noticed. The receptionist went in the back, to the bathroom, I suppose, and I said goodbye to him, but instead of leaving I went upstairs. I only intended to get my own photograph but then somebody came in. In the end I took the whole packet and ran.'

'And then you thought of getting rid of the necklace?'

'Later. I thought of throwing it in the river but if somebody had seen me . . . I wanted to put it back in the room, to undo what I'd done. And I knew you couldn't have looked in her hiding place or you'd have seen the photographs. I was too scared to try and sell it, anyway. Does my wife know?'

'Yes.'

'She'll be better off without me.' He didn't mention the little girl.

When they took him away the embarrassed young lawyer stood up and looked about him uncertainly, as if wondering whether he should shake hands with some of the others who were present, but since only the Marshal noticed his hesitation he left with a vague 'good morning' addressed to nobody in particular and unheard by anyone.

The Substitute dismissed his registrar, indicated the chairs opposite his desk to the Captain and Guarnaccia, and sat looking at them, his hands clasped beneath his chin. Maestrangelo was in no hurry to explain himself. He took time first to observe the raised eyebrows, the slightly pursed lips, and decided that the Substitute was more amused than annoyed. It was stupidity and dullness that annoyed him, not cleverness, and he was well aware of just how clever the Captain had been, Maestrangelo was sure of that. For not only had he produced the solution to the Querci case, he had engineered things in such a way as to put one over on the Substitute himself and had made Guarnaccia the protagonist so as to disarm him in the case of a complaint from Sweeton's father.

The two men looked at each other. The Marshal looked at his knees.

'Was there any problem with the English judge?' inquired the Captain, as though nothing of note had transpired in the last half-hour. Which amused the Substitute even more.

'No,' he said, pausing to glance at the Marshal, 'there wasn't. The boy explained the circumstances of his little accident to his father in my presence. He's now out of hospital and both he and his father are prepared to remain here until such time as we call the boy as a witness. And now, if it wouldn't be asking too much, perhaps you'd tell me something about the case in which he *is* a witness. I'm a little vague on that point.'

'The Becker case,' replied the Captain equably. 'You'll have my report in a few days.'

'Ah. A double homicide, I take it. And do we have a motive?'

'Suppression of witnesses, sir.'

'Suppression of witnesses. Witnesses to what? Maestrangelo, you don't have another corpse tucked away that you haven't found time to mention to me?'

'No, sir. I don't.'

'Good. You seem to me to be capable of anything—though perhaps it's the Marshal here I should be asking.'

The Marshal only raised his big eyes and stared at him in silent incomprehension. The Substitute abandoned his flippant tone.

'Well, Captain? Witnesses to what?'

'Theft, sir. Or rather, a series of thefts perpetrated in thirteen European cities over a period of approximately twelve years.' He took a telex from his pocket. 'I got in touch with Interpol early this morning. That's a very brief summary, the full information should come through later today.'

The Substitute glanced at the telex and then put it to one side. 'You'd better begin at the beginning.'

The Captain began in Mainz, with the highly intelligent, cold-blooded practical joker who liked an audience and who had openly kept two mistresses.

'He and the two women left Mainz, not together and not at exactly the same time but all within a year. Hilde Vogel came to Florence, where she hoped to settle with her father. The other woman whose name was Ursula Janz we know nothing of. According to rumours among the people of Mainz, Becker went either to New York or to Amsterdam. My guess is that it was Amsterdam, that he already had his new life planned. He had dealt in jewellery for years and knew his stuff. He needed to learn cutting.'

'If that's true, it won't be difficult to check.'

'In the eight years or so that this case has been on file at Interpol I imagine that the police of the countries concerned must have tried to check. Whoever taught him would have been very highly paid for both his skill and his discretion. And judging by Becker's recent form, I doubt if the cutter was allowed to outlive his usefulness.

'Once he had the skills he needed Becker's method was very simple. He would enter a jeweller's shop and choose a stone which he wanted to have set for his "wife". He knew the jewellery business and would talk with the jeweller at some length. He was well dressed, distinguished-looking, intelligent and eminently respectable. Having ascertained the weight and cut of the stone and examined it carefully he would leave, promising to return in a day or so with his wife. Then he would make a copy of the stone. Back in the shop, the original stone would pass from the jeweller to Becker to the wife. The stone they passed back was the false one. Becker and his wife would leave the shop to arrange for payment through a bank, perfectly normal since no one carries that sort of cash about and a cheque from an unknown person wouldn't be accepted. In some cases the theft wasn't discovered for many weeks, in one case it was six months. It all depended on when that particular stone came to be sold or set.'

'Hm . . .' The Substitute leant back a little in his chair and thought for a moment. 'What makes you so sure Becker's your man?'

'A number of things. His accomplices, first of all. As you see from the telex, there must have been two of them, in some instances a tall blonde, in others a small dark-haired woman. In each case the accomplice was fluent in the language of the country where the theft took place. We don't know about all Hilde Vogel's trips over the last twelve years but the ones we do know about coincide with thefts in those countries. It's probable that she was fluent in French as well as Italian. We know from Querci's statement that the other woman in Becker's life spoke perfect English. That stuck in my mind, I must say, since it seemed an odd thing to be so jealous about.'

'He must have paid them well—they couldn't have had much of a life, these women.'

'In my opinion, sir, he had a much stronger hold on them than just money. They must both have been in love with him and perhaps even afraid of him. Not only did they have no life of their own because of working for him, they had to tolerate each other's existence, as they had all those years ago in Mainz. Obviously money came into it too. Hilde Vogel hadn't enough to live on when she left home and her father had nothing and didn't want her anyway.'

'A strange life to choose, even so.'

'She had nothing else. Then her son turned up.'

'And Becker killed him, in your opinion?'

'Yes. She must have confessed everything to the boy. We know from John Sweeton that Christian was sure of getting a large amount of money from her because of something he knew about her. By the time Becker turned up, having received her letter saying she wanted to break with him, she was frightened enough and, I suppose, upset enough to tell him what she'd done and let him take over. The day after Christian's death, the morning after, to be exact, Becker walked into a jeweller's shop on the Ponte Vecchio, returned there two days later with his accomplice and committed another theft.'

'A remarkably cool character, if this is all true.'

'Whoever did those thefts had to be remarkable in many ways. It was the description of Becker's character that made me suspect him.'

'Well it's a convincing enough story, but why kill Hilde Vogel? And why a month later?'

'I don't know why he killed her. We may never know. As for why a month later, that could just be to leave a gap between that and the theft. If so, he was unfortunate because the two stories broke together. Not that anyone noticed at the time.'

'This jeweller, can he identify the Vogel woman?'

'I saw him this morning on my way here. I showed him her photograph.'

'And . . .?'

'Nothing. He's not sure. He remembers her being tall and blonde and very talkative—that would be to distract him while Becker passed him the counterfeit jewel, no doubt. But it was summer and she was wearing sunglasses. He can't remember her face at all.'

'I see.'

The Substitute picked up the telex again and looked at it in silence. The Marshal had sat patiently through this conversation he didn't consider himself competent even to think about. Now he glanced surreptitiously at his watch.

'All in all,' the Substitute said at last, 'we haven't a scrap of evidence against this man, have we?'

'No, sir,' replied the Captain, 'and we probably never will have. He still has another accomplice and there's nothing to prevent him from carrying on for many more years.'

'Well, send me your written report. All we can do is to keep the file open and wait for developments. Is the mother-in-law still here?'

'Until tomorrow—that is, if you're willing to release the boy's body.'

'I don't see why not. What about the woman's body? Surely if it's her daughter-in-law . . .?'

'I don't think she wants to take it back to Germany. She may change her mind, of course.'

'Arrange for me to see her tomorrow, will you? I may as well tell Sweeton he can take his son home. I don't think he's going to be needed as a witness for some time, if ever.'

The Captain said nothing. He and the Marshal got to their feet. Outside on the steps of the Procura the two of them stood for a moment beneath the great baroque façade, watching the traffic streaming by in the rain. The guard on duty hitched up his submachine-gun and gave them a brief salute.

'I'd give a lot to know why he killed Hilde Vogel,' the Captain said, putting on his hat, 'Even if we never find him.'

But the Marshal was thinking about Querci.

'I have to get off,' he said, 'I'm picking my wife up at the station.'

And they made a dash through the rain to their cars.

The Marshal lay in bed, his eyes wide open. He could hear his wife still moving about in the next room. His mind rambled over the events of the day and sometimes further back. He could hear the rain still falling heavily on the trees and gravel outside and imagined it filling the ditch that ran down from the fort to the dark swollen river. The thought made him shiver. What was his wife finding to do all this time? She had been busy from the moment she arrived, unpacking boxes full of tomato preserve, jam and fresh oranges and lemons. He'd have done better to take the van to meet her instead of his little Fiat. She had filled the kitchen to overflowing within minutes and had begun to cook immediately. Three or four times he had found an excuse to leave his office and come through to see what she was doing.

'You're getting in my way, whatever do you want this time?'

'A glass of water.' The first thing that came into his head, just like a little boy!

After supper he had pretended to read the newspaper, sneaking a glance at her every so often as she worked on a red sweater she was knitting for one of the boys, pausing occasionally to spread the piece over one knee and stroke it flat with her fingers, looking for non-existent mistakes.

Once she caught him watching her and smiled. 'It'll be different when the boys get here.'

And he had been embarrassed.

At last he heard her switch the sitting-room light off.

'You're in bed already!'

She began getting undressed, first removing her little string of artificial pearls.

'Do you always do that?' he asked her suddenly.

'Do what?'

'Take your pearls off before undressing?'

'Of course. Why?'

'Nothing. I just wondered . . .'

'What a funny thing to ask. Do you think I should go to the school first thing tomorrow?'

'If you do, you should go to the post office first and pay

their insurance and registration fees. I've got the forms in my desk.'

'You'll have to tell me where the post office is. What did they say at the school, exactly?'

'That all the sections studying English were full. They're the most popular. There's only room in the French sections.'

'Well, it's out of the question for them to change languages now. I'll see if I can convince them tomorrow . . . You should have been more insistent . . .'

And after a while, talking of other things, the Marshal forgot to listen to the rain that went on falling through the night into the dark water.

CHAPTER 12

There was another theft nine months later. This time it was Birmingham, in England. Both Becker and his one remaining accomplice had disappeared without trace by the time the stone concerned was discovered to be false some two weeks later. Since it was summer and nothing newsworthy was happening in Florence, Galli wrote a long, mostly hypothetical story in the *Nazione* with the headline, KILLER-THIEF STRIKES AGAIN. There was a picture of Hilde Vogel, the one the Captain had provided in the hope of identifying her, and one of Mario Querci with the sub-heading, *The one man who knows the face of the world-famous jewel thief.*

For Querci it was the end.

Galli had traced him, after some difficulty. He had just come out of prison and was living in a hostel. He had only got a six-month sentence, and since he had already served nine months before his case came up he was released immediately. When Galli found him he was penniless, for although in theory he had inherited all Hilde Vogel's money, the bulk of it remained in Switzerland, blocked because of the continuing investigation of the Vogel-Becker affair. In any case, as an Italian citizen he could not have imported it. The villa, which he had also inherited, was up for sale, but being so large and so rundown had found no buyer. It stood empty and rapidly decaying. The small amount of money in Hilde Vogel's account in Florence was at first confiscated and then released to cover payment of the rates on the villa and Avvocato Heer's fees. Galli gave Querci a small fee for his interview.

The day after the story appeared Querci turned up at Borgo Ognissanti looking for the Captain, with some garbled story about asking for protection. The Captain was out on a case and the guard on duty didn't recognize him. Querci was drunk anyway on the money the journalist had given him and the guard sent him away. The following week he turned up at the newspaper offices and tried to get in to see the editor. The editor was in a meeting. He asked for Galli, but Galli had gone away on holiday. In the end, a very young reporter who had nothing much else to do that day took pity on him and listened to his story for almost an hour, promising afterwards to talk to the editor about publishing a story claiming that Querci should be given police protection. He said it to make the unfortunate man feel better. He wouldn't have dared to do it since he had only been on the paper a month.

Somehow or other the Captain got to hear about Querci's visit and telephoned Guarnaccia.

'See if you can find him. They say in the paper he was staying in the hostel in Via Sant'Agostino when Galli talked to him but he's gone from there. You could try the others.'

'Do you think he's genuinely frightened?'

'Probably, if he believed that exaggerated story of Galli's. Even if he's not, he obviously needs some help. Some sort of work, for a start.'

'I should be able to do something there. I've been trying to find him anyway. His wife's been to see me. The family doesn't know, of course, but she wants to see him. If we can fix him up with some sort of job, they might manage to get on their feet again.'

'Well, keep a lookout. If he turns up here I'll send him over to you.'

Two weeks went by and nothing was heard of Querci. When Galli came back from his holiday the Captain telephoned him and gave him hell. Galli was genuinely remorseful.

'I thought the poor beggar needed money. I had to make a good story of it or I'd never have got it through on my expenses. I'll see if I can find him.'

'You do that.'

'I'll find him, don't worry. He's had a bad deal, poor sod. I was only trying to help him.'

It took Galli three days to track him down to where he was boarding illegally in a rundown house belonging to a woman who had three other undeclared lodgers, two of whom were smalltime crooks. When Galli spoke to her he didn't say who he was in case it should frighten Querci off. He called the Captain, who sent Guarnaccia to the house. Querci wasn't there, so he left a message. Instead of delivering it, the landlady, who couldn't afford to have the carabinieri nosing round the place, kicked Querci out as soon as he turned up.

At five o'clock on the following afternoon there were crowds of witnesses around to see a shabby-looking man, afterwards described as 'looking dazed', make straight for the parapet of the San Niccolò bridge and throw himself over without a moment's hesitation. Two of them jumped in after him and managed to drag him to the bank, but it was midsummer and the Arno was very low. Querci's head had struck the foundations of the bridge and he was dead in seconds from the blow.

The one person he had never considered asking for help was the Marshal, who had been responsible for sending him to prison.

*

It may have been because relations had remained cool ever since Mario Querci's death that Galli telephoned Maestrangelo the minute he got the news. Not only because he was a valued contact but because he liked and respected the man. And anyway, keeping one ahead of the usual press conferences by the use of a short-wave radio instead of through having a good contact was as unsatisfactory as it was illegal.

'I thought you'd like to know,' he announced one fine spring morning the following year, 'that we've got the whole story on Walter Becker—you remember him?—Thefts, murders, everything.'

'You mean they've caught him?' The Captain was almost disappointed, not at the idea of some other Force catching his man but because he had come to think of Becker as a sort of invincible super-criminal.

'No, they haven't caught him,' Galli said, 'or you'd have heard before I did. He's dead. Died of a stroke at his home in New York a few days ago. But it seems he couldn't bear to leave us without being sure that his great genius was fully appreciated by the world. He had deposited the full details of his successful life of crime with his lawyer, to be sent to an important German newspaper on his death. A contact of mine on this paper has written the story up and sent the documents on to me. I'm writing it up now. As soon as I've finished this evening I could send the stuff over to you. That's if you're interested.'

'I am. Thank you. But is there any explanation of why he killed the Vogel woman?'

Galli chuckled. 'That's easy. He killed the other accomplice too, one month after that last theft in England. Hilde Vogel's death had nothing to do with that business of the son. The reason was simple enough: Becker was fifty-five.'

'Fifty-five . . .?'

'Exactly. He retired!'

As soon as the package of papers arrived, towards eight

in the evening, Maestrangelo cleared his desk and asked not
to be disturbed unless there was something urgent.

There were reams of it. Stacks of closely written pages in
a tiny, fanatically neat script, red underlinings, numbered
lists. It was frustrating not to be able to read the originals
which were in German, but Galli had attached the roughly
typed translation he'd had done for his article. The lists concerned the stones Becker had stolen. They were divided into
columns showing carat weight, cut, clarity, colour, the date
of the theft and the cost of making the false replica, the
recutting and sale of the original, with calculations on the
loss of value involved in cutting a large stone into smaller
ones. The loss was evidently considerable, often a little more
than fifty percent of the original weight, and in most cases
Becker had succeeded in selling the original untouched
because the theft hadn't been discovered. These sales were
recorded as having been made in Antwerp.

On a separate sheet, enormous and folded into four, was
a master plan drawn up over an outline map of Europe.
Cities where thefts were to take place were circled in green
ink and numbered. The accomplice's initials were written
next to the number in black. Beside the cities of Florence in
Italy and Birmingham in England the initials were circled
in blue. This plan had evidently been drawn up by Becker
at the very beginning of his career since the paper was
yellowish and split on the folds and the ink was faded.
Including the blue circles round the initials. The deaths of
the two women were planned, almost to the minute, all
those years ago. A third set of initials was circled in blue
beside the city of Amsterdam. That must have been the
cutter who had taught him his craft. The rest of the sheets
formed a sort of diary, but a diary that wasn't written for
the diarist himself but for a public, for the audience Becker
always had to have. His only real weakness and one he knew
well how to control.

In Amsterdam he had written:

I have learnt in less than two years what would normally take at least five. The old man himself told me so today. He has no sons and I do believe he's nursing a sentimental hope that I will stay on and take over from him. This sort of sentimental wishful thinking now causes him to hide from himself what he knows must be my real reason for being here, just as greed caused him to hide it from himself at the beginning. He will continue to deceive himself up to the moment of his 'suicide' because that is what he wishes. As always, my role is an entirely passive one . . .

Of Hilde Vogel he had written:

Encouraging H.'s attempts to seek out her father was as necessary as encouraging her marriage to C. Her dependence on and submission to me frightened her at the beginning and any attempt to enforce them might have resulted in her escaping me. Now she is resigned to her situation. Only the timing was difficult. U. is in London and we are ready to start work. Without H. it would have been more difficult, not only because of languages but because neither will ever retire from the scene as long as the other is there. If anything unforeseen should occur and one of them tries to back out, the other could in theory start to blackmail. I have been careful to implant this idea while offering comforting assurances that it couldn't happen . . .

And when the unforeseen did occur:

H. created a dangerous mess. She now believes the boy took the cash and left, which is what she wishes to believe. Tomorrow we go ahead as planned since the boy's death is irrelevant, as H.'s would not be were she recognized. A month should create sufficient space. Let us hope that no similar mess awaits me in England with my last piece of work.

Presumably it hadn't. Presumably, when this news filtered through via Interpol, some English policeman would insert the name Ursula Janz into the file regarding an unidentified body, close the file and send it to the archives.

Just as the Captain could now close the Vogel-Becker file. He stared across at the window without seeing the evening sunshine flooding the stones of the building opposite with a soft pink light. *That foreigner in a fur coat job.*

That was how the case was still remembered. It somehow seemed likely that it would go on being remembered that way, even after the big splash Becker's story would make in tomorrow's paper. What did that mean? Was it one up on Becker that Hilde Vogel's story remained hers and not just a sub-plot of his? Or did it only emphasize how clever he had been about separating the two in the first place? One thing was certain: Becker knew how to manipulate the Press. There was a note from Galli on the envelope the stuff came in saying that there were photographs, too. Of Becker, his accomplices and the more spectacular of the jewels, real and false. The note said these were still at the paper being prepared for tomorrow's publication. The complete Press handout. If the man had tried his hand at journalism he would have been brilliant at that, too. Or at anything else.

Ninety-nine point nine per cent of people are fools.

Querci hadn't known how to manipulate the Press. A poor survivor, a born victim, in Becker's terms a fool.

The last words Becker had written were on a separate sheet.

This is my first day in retirement. If I have any regrets it is only because most of it has been too easy. The only real difficulty was getting myself accepted here in New York where I sold many of the stones. It took a long time to infiltrate the Diamond Dealers' Club. Even with the introduction I got the old man to write for me. Most of the dealers are Orthodox Jews and everything is done on trust among them. Thousands of dollars' worth of stones change hands on W. 47th Street with no more collateral than a handshake. It was some time before they bought from me and then cautiously. But demand always succeeds supply in this business and in the end

they accepted my presence and bought more, but I never became one
of them. Only between themselves do they conclude a deal by rising
and saying with a clasp of hands mazel und broche. *They are*
the only people I encountered who presented a worthy challenge.

I never gave any serious thought to the possibility of getting
caught, never used a false name or papers, never left the 'scene of
the crime' in haste. There was no necessity for it. The police
are trained to seek out weakness, passion, greed, stupidity, not
intelligence and objectivity. This, of course, is as it should be.

As it should be.
'A madman,' Maestrangelo said aloud, and then shrugged
his shoulders as though to rid himself of Becker's influence.
He thought of ringing Guarnaccia to let him know, but on
second thoughts he found he had no desire to talk about
this business and probably the Marshal hadn't either.
In any case he would see it all tomorrow in the paper.

The Marshal didn't see it in the paper. At least he said he
hadn't when Lorenzini cautiously referred to it. Cautiously
because he remembered how the Marshal had been like a
bear with a sore head about that body they'd found in the
ditch up by the fort and then almost as bad about that
suicide last summer. Still, it was all long enough ago for
Lorenzini to risk remarking:
'Did you see Galli's article?'
'What article?'
'I thought I saw you reading it, the one about—'
'I'm not likely to get time to read the newspaper until
next October. What's happening about that lost child that's
been brought in?'
'We're still trying to trace the parents. She's obviously
foreign but she's so tiny and we can't work out what langu-
age she speaks, so—'
'Where's the report about that car?'
'You've got it in your hand, Marshal, I just gave it to
you . . .'

'Right. I'll be in my office. See to those people in the waiting-room, the woman's had her bag snatched, passport, traveller's cheques, the lot—and give her a glass of water, she's upset.'

And Lorenzini watched him stump off, papers in hand, to his office, grumbling under his breath as he did from Easter to September every year:

'I don't know what they come here for, they'd do better to stay at home . . .'

Fontana Paperbacks: Fiction

Fontana is a leading paperback publisher of both non-fiction, popular and academic, and fiction. Below are some recent fiction titles.

- [ ] SEEDS OF YESTERDAY Virginia Andrews £2.50
- [ ] SONG OF RHANNA Christine Marion Fraser £2.50
- [ ] JEDDER'S LAND Maureen O'Donoghue £1.95
- [ ] THE WARLORD Malcolm Bosse £2.95
- [ ] TREASON'S HARBOUR Patrick O'Brian £2.50
- [ ] FUTURES Freda Bright £1.95
- [ ] THE DEMON LOVER Victoria Holt £2.50
- [ ] FIREPRINT Geoffrey Jenkins £2.50
- [ ] DEATH AND THE DANCING FOOTMAN Ngaio Marsh £1.75
- [ ] THE 'CAINE' MUTINY Herman Wouk £2.50
- [ ] LIVERPOOL DAISY Helen Forrester £1.95
- [ ] OUT OF A DREAM Diana Anthony £1.75
- [ ] SHARPE'S ENEMY Bernard Cornwell £1.95

You can buy Fontana paperbacks at your local bookshop or newsagent. Or you can order them from Fontana Paperbacks, Cash Sales Department, Box 29, Douglas, Isle of Man. Please send a cheque, postal or money order (not currency) worth the purchase price plus 15p per book for postage (maximum postage required is £3).

NAME (Block letters) _____

ADDRESS _____

_____

_____